LUCKNOW MY LUCKNOW

Jagdish Arora

KALPAZ

Lucknow My Lucknow

₹ 565/-

ISBN: 978-93-5128-031-6

Published in 2014 in India by
Kalpaz Publications
C-30, Satyawati Nagar,
Delhi-110052
E-mail: kalpaz@hotmail.com

Laser Typesetting : Rudra Computer Graphics, Delhi
Printed at : G. Print Process, Delhi

Feelings to Suffer alone paying the cost
for my love's soothe

Contents

Luknow My Lucknow

That name still conjures up visions of the Nawabs with their splendid retinues and their magnificent palaces throbbing with life. The Splendor of the city's culture is reflected in its subtle fusion of sophistication and emotional warmth, its language, and the manners of its people. Its greatest attraction lies in its art of accepting the old and assimilating the new.

HOW TO REACH

By Air

Choudhry Charan Singh Airport, Lucknow, is directly connected with Delhi, Patna, Kolkata, Mumbai and Varanasi by direct flights.

By Rail

A major railway junction, Lucknow, is conveniently connected to many cities. Some of the important trains are :

Shatabdi Exp., Awadh Exp., Sabarmati Exp., Vaishali Exp., Avadh Assam Exp., Neelanchal Exp., Ganga Yamuna Exp., Lucknow Mail, Gomti Exp., Kashi-Vishwanath Exp., Nauchandi Exp., Bombay-Gorakhpur Exp., Cochin-Gorakhpur Exp.

By Road

Lucknow is connected by road with all the major cities of the country.

Some of the major road distances are

Agra	-	363 km
Allahabad	-	210 km
Ayodhya	-	135 km
Kolkata	-	985 km
Corbett National Park	-	400 km
Delhi	-	497 km
Dudhwa National Park	-	238 km
Kanpur	-	79 km
Khajuraho	-	320 km
Varanasi	-	305 km

GENERAL INFORMATION

Area	:	79 sq. kms.
Population	:	3647834 (2001 census)
Altitude	:	123 mtr. above sea level
Best Season	:	October-March
Clothing	:	Summer : Cottons Winter : Wollens
Languages	:	Hindi, Urdu, English
Local Transport	:	Bus/Tempo/Auto-rickshaw/ Taxi/Tonga/Cycle-ricksaw
STD Code	:	0522
G.P.O. Pincode	:	226001

Foreword

Welcome to Lucknow, you are in a city that typified like no other place in India has ever done, the very quintessence of this Country culture. We are the city where skyscrapers over look the *nawabi* culture, where parks flank bustling shopping districts, where animated neighbourhood thrive among cosmopolitan communities and where culture abounds, from cultural activities from theater to Kathak Dance to street festivals. This unique mix of global attractions and local charm makes visitor to Lucknow an unforgettable experience. They say you don't truly know some one until you have walked a mile in there shoes. The same goes for a city.

The best of India is right here - best restaurants, best clubs, best meeting and convention spaces and mainly Lucknow culture and more and more.

Lucknow is open year a round. I encourage you to explore this magnificent city and on behalf of all Lucknowites, we look forward to welcoming you again and again. Enjoy your visit and we hope to see you again and again.

It is a city that figures prominently on country's map of the first War of Independence era, having been geographically, of that grim sporadic struggle. An excursion to the Lucknow Residency would bear out incontrovertibly the veracity of the city's significance in the annals of Indian History.

The newcomer would still discern a unique appeal in the far flung parks and gardens of Lucknow, in the solemn grandeur of the Imperious Imambaras and in the occult majesty of the treacherous Gomti.

Broadly speaking the truest specimens of all that is old-time Lucknow or rather "Nucklow" as Rudyard Kipling chose to call it in his immortal stories, are to be found in the western parts of the city. In the eastern areas, while they form by themselves no less an attraction of Lucknow, the stamp of impact of modern society with its natural sophistications of both architecture and industry would be more evident. These, however, have so far in no manner impaired the overall conservative image of Lucknow where language, customs and culture are concerned.

A night's travel by train divides Lucknow and Delhi, which have between them a 510 kilometers span. Mumbai is some good 1,450 odd kilometers' away from Lucknow.

Summer in Lucknow are quite sultry with the mercury shooting up to 45 degrees Celsius, while the rigours of wintry nights here are equally frightful, unless one uses sufficient Layers. The monsoons are on the whole, what they are usually expected to be rather moderate and sometime unbearable. Celsius named after the Swedish astronomers Andres Celsius.

First training armored corps training center was in Lucknow and Lucknow has one of the best cantonments with Headquarters central command located here.

Col. P.G. Roy
(Retd.)

Preface

Lucknow: A truly diverse and dynamic destination perched with its feet firmly etched in old world etiquette yet a vision spanning towards a bright modern future. A city that has something to offer for everyone, as a multi cultural and cosmopolitan capital of Uttar Pradesh, the most populous state of India. A city that has a magical charm, a charm that's forever and a charm that's apart. Be it the cultural charm or the monumental one, all are well conserved here to make Lucknow "The city of many splendors".

As the seat of the government of Uttar Pradesh, Lucknow is the site of the Vidhan Sabha, the High Court and numerous government departments. Lucknow has several educational and research organisations like La Martiniere College, IIM Lucknow, Central Drug Research Institute, National Botanical Research Institute, Dr. Ram Manohar Lohia National Law University, Sanjay Gandhi Post Graduate Institute of Medical Sciences, King George Medical College and Loretto Convent. It is the birth place and breeding ground of many social and cultural institutions of national significance, such as the Kathak, Khayal, Urdu Poetry and Classical music.

The surviving monuments of the city mark the evolution of totally different style in architecture. During the Nawabi era - the Mughal legacy was reinterpreted in stone and stucco and soon the builders began to experiment with European styles and attempts were made to fuse the occidental with the oriental. The style that emerged could rival the best in the world. Modern city of Lucknow, spread evenly on both sides of the Gomti, offers a tourist plenty of places of historical interest. Old monuments, parks and markets vie for space with sprawling new malls. Aminabad, with its twisted lanes, is the main shopping centre, though Hazratganj, with its theatres, coffee houses, restaurants, hotels and bars has attracted tourists since long.

Walking through the lanes and by-lanes of Chowk and Aminabad one finds the Lucknow of yore. The 'tehzeeb' or mannerism is still prominent and greatly appreciated. This is a city that still speaks the language of "aap-janab" and the dictum of "pehle aap" is still a part of everyday life for every Lakhnawi. Dress forms have changed noticeably in the span of a century, yet the beauty and charisma of Chikan, Zardozi and Mukaish - the various types of intricate and delicate hand embroidery, still command place in the wardrobe. It is a city where the 'Khansaamas' of olden times are still remembered amid the ever growing hustle-bustle of retail chain coffee shops and fine dine(s) serving global haute cuisine.

Today, Lucknow is a vibrant city that is witnessing an economic boom and is among the top ten fastest growing non-major-metropolitan cities of India. It is the second largest city in Uttar Pradesh state. The unique combination of its cultured grace and newly acquired pace is its most promising feature that augurs well for the future.

Muskuraiye ki aap Lucknow mein hain!!

Rajnish Chopra

Introduction

As an author, I have numerous publications to my credit. I have ventured to write on various issues from culture, social, sports and topics which can tantalize readers of all walks of life. About LUCKNOW, my association is right from my university days and since then I had been member of various clubs and institutions associating myself with the cities vibrant culture. My old time bosom friend Late Prem Bhatia, was the one to guide to me write this book on Lucknow.

It would be unkind of me in case as a tribute to the soul of my friend Prem, I fail to write something about him. Popularly called Prem by one and all, he was a bundle of joy and friend of friends. No club around the corner could miss Prem's absence and be it poor or rich, every one had only one word for him "JUST GREAT" I had been very lucky to have a friend in him. No evening would be complete without his company. Those were not the days of mobile and even telephone savvy. Our telephones were more than often out of service due to poor maintenance. Prem would send across his servant all the way to confirm programmes in case the telephone was out of order. He being no more physically with us, a futile wait is on, case some other friend like him could fix an evening with them. But where to find a friend of his stature! All those who knew him must be in same boat as I am in, waiting for a call or a small SMS now.

It was Prem who forced me to write a book on Lucknow. Since I had been actively associated with almost all activities from sports to film and offers a unique opportunity to discovers culture of Lucknow, inspiration from Prem acted as a catalyst, and thus I could present this book in front of you. The book in this present form has a number of esteemed individuals who have helped me to write it in this form. I must thank Mr. Bhupesh Bhatia, Mr. Rohin Arora and Lt. Col. Kuldip Singh (Retd.), Mr. Rajnish Chopra and Mr. Pranabesh Das Gupta.

Hope you enjoy rea ding this book and get a first hand knowledge of Lucknow, the capital of one time Awadh, and thank Prem Bhatia in case the book is able to make you happy even in a small way. We look forward to welcoming you again. This unique mix global attractions local local charm makes visiting Lucknow an forgettable experience.

Jagdish Arora

108, 1st Floor, Block A
Empire Estate Residency
Mall Avenue, Lucknow-226001

1

Lucknow History and Tehzeeb

Lucknow has several landmarks that honour the achievements of Lucknow's brightest stars. From hockey greats to world renowned musicians, poets, actors, directors, the country's notables are commemorated throughout the city.

Lucknow or Nucklow is a superb city, often surpassing many European capitals for its heritage, beauty, art and culture. Even before the arrival of the Nawabi dynasty, Lucknow had the settlements of Firangi Mahal to its credit and many other noteworthy monuments and buildings. Then there are *dhabas* Indian excellence and Mughlai Restaurants all offer sophisticated menus featuring cuisine from host of regions. With so much choice, its just a matter of taste where you choose to go. A one-stop spot Saharaganj for every thing great in Lucknow with details on dining, attractions, shopping and events. See Lucknow is the essential for navigating the abundance of cool things to see and do in the city, it has nifty features like searchable restaurants listings to point the way to nearby eateries. Make your trip in and around the city feel like home.

Lucknow, which today comprises the old and the new, belongs to the Mughal Period when the fourth Nawab Asaf-ud-Daula (1775-1797), shifted his seat of power from Faizabad to Lucknow in the year 1775. The Nawab directed all his available resources to build a city of his dreams, brick by brick, like no other city in India that ever existed. The Bara Imambara and the Rumi Darwaza and the monuments of Lucknow, herald the uniqueness of the city and reflect its rich cultural heritage. These monumental edifices speak volumes about Nawab Asaf-ud-Daula's zeal, passion and love for his newly built city of Lucknow.

The virtue to appreciate all that was beautiful in art, architecture, music, humanities, culture, nature and language was the driving force that created legendary Lucknow. After the construction of royal palaces, villas, gardens and country homes, places of worship, memorials and monuments, a need arose for their connectivity. Dilkusha, the Kothi Hayat Baksh, the Kothi Nur Bakhsh, and Farhat Bakhsh Palace, a wide road was laid down in the year 1810 in the reign of the sixth Nawab, Nawab Saadat Ali Khan (1798-1814) his cousin Nawab Asaf-ud-Daula. Construction was under the supervision of Raja Bakhtawar Singh, who was born near Baksar and subsequently acquired land holdings around Ayodhya. With the passage of time this road has undergone many changes in its course and nomenclature. The road from Kothi Hayat Bakhsh (now Raj Bhawan) to Farhat Bakhsh adjacent to Chatar Manzil (now the Central Drug Research Institute) and passing through the Hazratganj market was, during the British Raj called the Mall or Queen's way. Post-independence it has been named Mahatma Gandhi Road by the Govt. of Chief Minister Mr. G.B. Pant.

If Lucknow was the Paris of India, the heart of this enthralling magnificent city undoubtedly lies beating in Hazratganj. Recognised as the epitome of art, culture, elegance, sophistication and beauty, it is presently celebrating 200 years of its existence. Recently fully renovated and spruced up with lighted fountains, Victorian-style ornated lamp post and the cobbled promenade, with lush green spots to complement the restored facades, it is an ambitious attempt to restore back its past glory. The credit goes to Ms. Mayawati (known as Behanji with respect), Ex-Chief Minister of Uttar Pradesh. What people miss in Hazratganj are Mayfair Cinema, Kwality Restaurant and Modern Novelties. The capital of Uttar Pradesh, Lucknow's weather is tempered by River Gomti, which softens the winter bite and ease the summer heat.

A series of palaces forming a huge complex built by Amjad Ali Shah, in 1844 and gifted to one of his wife Queen Malka Ahad was called the Begum Kothi. Within it stood the Kothi Inayat Sultan. This complex comprised a large area at the very core of Hazratganj, occupying a vast area extending from the existing Shahi Masjid on today's Vidhan Sabha Marg till the boundaries of Imambara Sibtainabad Mubarak. This royal complex was self sufficient in its layout having its own mosque, imambaras.

Hazratganj was not actually named as such until the early 1850s. Before that it was simply described as Horses Tabela. Its name probably came, we have seen, from the mausoleum of 'Hazrat-Mahal'. Victoria Park is changed to Hazrat Mahal Park.

It seems clear that before the British takeover of Awadh, and its capital Lucknow, in 1857, the visitor moved around between different areas, not along named roads. Someone going to Rakabganj, for example, would simply set out along the road that lead to this particular mohalla, without needing the name of the road that took him there. Much of Lucknow was named either on the person who owned a particular piece of land, like Tikaitganj, after Maharaja Tikait Rai or from particular occupations and inhabitants of a certain area. 'Sabzi Mandi' was clearly the vegetable market, 'Chobdari Mohalla' the place where the mace-bearers lived, and the curiously named 'Gend Khana Jadeed' was new area for ball games, most probably a racquet court. 'Nakhas' was originally the horse- market, and Gau Ghat the river area where cattles went to drink water.

It was the British rule who gave many of Lucknow's roads their first names after annexation in 1857. The idea that identifying and naming streets was particular tool of colonial power is not a new one.

Now it is worth pointing out that although we commemorate some of the great names in Indian history with Rani Laxmi Bai, Rana Pratap, Shivaji Maharaj, Tipu Sultan, Nana Saheb, Tantiya Tope, where are the names of the men who actually created Lucknow. There is no mention in history book, except Nawab Asaf-ud-Daula.

Lucknow is a city of cultures, religions and languages each individually so refined that it emanates an aroma of love, respect, humility and compassion. Now the Hazratganj is looking good with arcades. A city known to the country for its 'Tahzeeb', heritage and culture. A city once referred to as the literary capital of India, a centre point of the Urdu language, a city which prided itself on the respect for others, respect for all religions and elders - Lucknow is a city of multi-faceted religions and languages, bound together by one language- the language of the heart and love and affection.

Lucknow has a culture, it has history, heritage and above all adventure which makes its position unique in our country, India.

The completion of 200 years of Hazratganj was a perfect opportunity to rekindle the past, an opportunity to refocus attention to this great vibrant city, an opportunity to showcase this city's *tehzeeb*, an opportunity to preserve and pass on this great heritage seem to have become oblivious of what Lucknow stood for and what it was- as Kipling called lucknow. Villagers still call it Lucknow.

Tourists from all over the world who visited Lucknow are still fascinated by this loveable city which has caught their admiration, amazement and those connected with this part of the world often go into a nostalgic tizzy at the mention of 'Ganjing'.

Hazratganj is whatever it is thanks to being a part of this inherently vibrant and warm city of Tehzeeb. We have all inherited a culture which not only does us proud but also gives us a responsibility to not only maintain what we have inherited but also try and spread it as far and wide as possible.

Eminent citizens, like Lord Khalid Hameed of Hapstead, Padma Shri Dr. Mansoor Hasan, Shri Mizaffar Ali, Late B.N. Talwar, Late A.L. Sahni, Prem Tandon, Late Col. V.R. Mohan, Late C.B. Gupta Ramesh Tandon, Rai Bahadur Gurbux Singh, Dr. R.K. Pahuri, living legend Dr. Ashok Sharma, Rani Lila Ram Kumar Bhargava, Mr. (Late) Justice (Retd.) Uma Shanker Srivastava and Late Mayor Beni Pd. Halwasiya, Om Narayan Bansal, Begum Hamida Habibullah and Raj Bisaria and Late S.N. Ghosh (The Pioneer) Mr. Vinod Mehta, Lachhu Maharaj and K.D. Singh Babu.

In 1947, the British Raj was over. But the Raj lifestyle did not end with that one stroke of the midnight hour.

Like-minded citizens of Hazratganj got together and New Hazratganj was born. Requests were made to the government seeking its participation and with the full support of the U.P. Govt., the project took on a dimension like never before. The seed had been sown and new synergy had developed between Government, traders and like-minded people.

The Divisional Commissioner, Lucknow took charge and Mr. Asheesh Srivastava, an architect of stature in the field of heritage preservation and a man with a passion to transform Hazratganj was brought on board. Lucknow Nagar Nigam, Lucknow Development Authority, and Jal Sansthan started buzzing with activity. Regular meetings of like-minded citizens of Lucknow and district officials became a norm.

With the project gradually taking shape, the multilevel parking became an important part of the rejuvenation exercise. The old Kotwali bore the brunt and the century old structure was brought down to make way for the requirements of the coming decades. Though great care was taken to ensure that the facade of the structure blended with the archaic ambience of its neighbours, it did raise eyebrows and concerns which caved in to sustained reasoning. A rejuvenated Ganj with a committed parking would not only provide succor to the shoppers who went up and down. Hazratganj with new look was born and celebrated 200 years of its existence. Lucknow has malls at Shahnajaf Road, Gomti Nagar and at Kanpur Road. Go ahead and use Lucknow as a convenient hub from which to explore some of Lucknow's stellar attractions.

Then there are dhabas offering Indian excellence food known as Taste of India, and Muglai Restaurants all offer sophisticated menus featuring cuisine from host of the regions. 360 Restaurant is an inspiring gastronomic hub in an unsurpassed setting. With so much choice it is just a matter of taste where you choose to go. Saharaganj is a hot spot for everything great in Lucknow. With details on dining attractions, shopping and events. See Lucknow, it is the essential app for navigating the abounds once of cool things to see and do in the city.

Hazratganj is now known as ultra modern market, though the roots of the past run deep.

2

Monuments in Lucknow

After the conquest of Kannauj by the Afghans at the end of the 12th century, Awadh submitted to the Sultan of Ghazni and became a part of the Delhi empire and subsequently a subah (or province) of the Mughal empire. In 1526, Lucknow was temporarily occupied by the Mughal prince Humayun. In 1540, he lost the throne to his Afghan rival, Sher Shah, who occupied Lucknow where he established a copper mint. During the Mughal reign, Lucknow became a major center of commerce, which persuaded a French merchant to settle here. He reaped enough profits to build four splendid houses in the very first year, but was not given permission to stay further. His persistence resulted in the confiscation of his property, which came to be known as the Firangi Mahal.

The Legendary Tale

History has very little to say about the founders or the first settlers of Lucknow. According to a popular legend, Lord Ramchandra of Ayodhya, the hero of the famous epic Ramayana, gifted the territory of Lucknow to his devoted brother Lakshman after his victory over the demon king Ravana. The original name of Lucknow

is thus believed to be Lakshmanpur or Lakhanpur. Yet another story suggests that this city was a gift to the holy sages of this region by Lord Yudhishter's grandson.

The story of Lucknow, as we know today, begins in 1732 when Saadat Khan, a Persian adventurer, originally from Khurasan in Persia, was honored by the Mughal Emperor, Muhammad Shah, and was made Nizam or governor of the province of Avadh and later the Nawab. In 1740, the Nawab was called Wazir, which means Chief Minister- hence he was given the title Nawab Wazir. In practice from Sadat Khan onwards, titles have been hereditary, inheritors of which were responsible for shaping the history of Lucknow.

Lucknow Flourished under the Regime of Asaf-ud-Daulah

Nawab Saadat Khan was succeeded by his nephew and son-in-law Safdar Jung in 1814. It was his grandson Asaf-ud-Daulah, the fourth Nawab, who transferred the seat of the Awadh government to Lucknow in 1775, to distance himself from his imperious mother in Faizabad. Thereon ushered a new era.

Asaf-ud-Daulah

In the eight intense decades that followed (i.e. 1775-1856), Lucknow prospered and grew into a sophisticated and picturesque city with parks, palaces, gardens and imposing architectural monuments. The Nawab's patronage of music and arts attracted poets, artists, and musicians to Lucknow in large numbers. During these eventful years, Lucknow became one of the most celebrated centers of opulence, dance, poetry and scholarship.

Wajid Ali Shah

Bara Immambara

Bara Imambara

Asaf-ud-Daulah was also an inveterate builder of monuments. Driven with an ambition to discover the glory of the past and present and surpass them in magnificence and splendor, the numerous buildings built by Asaf-ud-Daulah, like the Bara Imambara built in 1784, testify to his architectural zeal.

This is indeed a monumental feat considering the fact that it once boasted of the largest vaulted hall in the world, with a 50 feet high roof, spanning an area of 162 feet and a height 53 feet in the absence of a single beam. After all, as per the Nawab's directive, his architecture was to be original in conception with no influence of any existing structure or design.

The galleries and corridors within the great Imambara form a complicated and intricate labyrinth (*bhool-bhulaiya*) through which at times it is difficult to find your way. Its terrace provides a fine view of the Lucknow city. During one of his visits to the site, the pleasing aroma of food being cooked in giant ovens attracted the Nawab. It is here when he discovered the *dam* process of cooking, wherein the food is cooked slowly in its own steam, which lends a unique aroma and flavor to the food. Impressed with the process, he ordered the royal kitchen to practice the same method of cooking.

Rumi Darwaza or the Turkish Gate

Towards the west of the Imambara is the Rumi Darwaza or the Turkish Gate built by Asaf-ud-Daulah between the years 1784 to 1786. The 60 feet high gateway stands as an equally grand entrance to the great hall. During the Nawabi era, a huge lantern placed atop the Rumi Darwaza would light up the pathway, while jets of water gushed from the numerous fountains created on the rim of the gateway.

Rumi Darwaza

While on one hand the Nawabs had achieved a certain degree of independence from the Moghuls in Delhi, they surrendered their hold over the years as allies to the British who were there in the form of the East India Company based in Calcutta. Asaf-ud-Dualah's son, Wazir Ali took over the throne after his father's death in 1798. After four months of misrule and bad behavior, the British removed Wajid Ali from the throne in 1798, who had by then acquired enough powers to manipulate the events of Awadh. Sadat Ali Khan, Asaf-ud-Daulah's brother, was offered the throne, who during his 16 years of reign, earned himself a reputation of being an able administrator and the most sagacious Nawab that Lucknow had ever known.

British Residency

Unlike his predecessor, Sadat Ali proved to be a great builder who introduced a large number of architectural styles. One of his best known monuments is the Residency, which was built in 1800 for the British Resident.

British Residency

Today it stands desolate as a mute witness to the Mutiny of 1857 when it was almost completely almost recreates the history associated with it and is a stark reminder of the numerous sieges during the Mutiny. Among the long list of grand palaces commissioned by Sadat Ali, the Moti Mahal, Dilkusha Palace, Hayat Baksh, Chattar Manzil, Khusheed Manzil and Lal Baradari, deserves a visit.

The Nawab Wazirs of Lucknow, dissatisfied with their present titles, wanted to be called Kings, which at that time only the Emperors of Delhi were entitled to have. In 1819, Gazi-ud-Din, son and successor of Sadat Ali was made the first king.

Gazi-ud-Din was a generous ruler, a good monarch who paid due attention to administration and justice. He was responsible for building public works of all kinds. His buildings include the Mubarak Mahal, Shah Manzil and the Hazari Bagh, in which he introduced to the society of Lucknow, the sport of animal combats for the first time.

Residency Inside

Shah Najaf Imambara

Gazi-ud-Din's most outstanding building is the Shah Najaf Imambara where he is entombed together with his three wives. The Imambara is a huge masonry structure with a large dome. The wise Nawab gave the British a large sum of money for its embellishment and maintenance.

Under the terms of agreement, this mausoleum is well cared for and is in excellent condition even today.

Tarunvali Kothi

Ironically, the proclamation of kingship coincided with a period of almost complete dependence on the British. The title of King neither improved the administrative capabilities of the rulers nor their morale. The second King Nasir-ud-Din Haider, son and successor of Gazi-ud-Din, was so effeminate that he often spoke and dressed like a female. His only contribution in the field of architecture was the construction of Tarunvali Kothi, an archeological center, which was equipped with sophisticated instruments and entrusted to the care of a British astronomer.

Muhammad Ali's Imambara

The British crowned the third king of Awadh, Muhammad Ali who was the second son of Nawab Wazir Sadat Ali, in 1837 at a ripe old age of 63. Muhammad Ali was just and popular ruler under whom Lucknow once again regained its splendor for a brief spell. Interested in building activities, he built his own Imambara as well as the Juma Masjid. The Imambara, left incomplete by Muhammad Ali, was later completed by Begum Mallika Jehan of the Royal family. Between the Imambara and the gateway is a large courtyard with a rectangular raised tank spanned by a bridge. Within the Imambara is the burial place of the king while his daughter and

Chota Imambara

son-in-law are buried on one side of the courtyard. The Imambara is noted for its golden dome; exquisite chandeliers, huge mirrors, silver mimbar, colourful interiors and delicate calligraphy on its arched entrance.

Juma Masjid

The Juma Masjid, with its two minarets and three domes is yet another delightful place to visit in Lucknow. An interesting building by Muhammed Ali Shah is the Baradari, also known as the Picture Gallery, which houses the portraits of the erstwhile, Nawabs and Kings of Awadh. Here one can admire the marvellous costumes and jewelry that the nobles adorned themselves with. A patient of chronic rheumatism, Muhammad Ali died in 1842 and left behind a number of incomplete monuments, which would have honored him as the greatest builders amongst all Awadh Kings. The Sat

Khanda (or seven slices) was an edifice planned to resemble the minaret of Babylon with each of its storeys superimposed on the other- the top of which was to provide one of the finest views of Lucknow. Not far from the picture gallery is yet another marvel, the Clock Tower which is said to be the largest in India. This was, however, completed in seven years at the cost of more than a lakh of rupees- an enormous amount at that time.

Qaiser Bagh Palace

Muhammed Ali was succeeded by his son, Wajid Ali Shah in 1837 who was also the last of the rulers to ascend the throne. A poet, singer and a great patron of arts, his pursuit of personal pleasure left little time for looking into administrative responsibilities. This led to the British annexation of Awadh. Wajid Ali Shah's single contribution to Lucknow was the Qaiser Bagh Palace built in 1850, which he wanted to be promoted as the eighth wonder of the world.

Qaiser Bagh Palace

La Martiniere-A Funerary Monument

The architectural skyline of Lucknow remains incomplete without the mention of La Martiniere a funerary monument. Built at the end of the 18th century, it is said to be the largest in Asia and houses the coffin of its builder, French Major General Claude Martin. Martin had come to India as a penniless soldier but gradually his luck and labour fetched him a fortune big enough to lend a princely amount of 250,000 pounds to the Nawab Asaf-ud-Daulah! La Martiniere is today a school of great repute.

Lucknow's Cultural History Remains

In almost all forms of art and entertainment, Lucknow developed its own variety, be it poetry, music, dance, story telling, fashion, animal combats and gastronomy. The Dastarkhans of the Lucknow courts are still proverbial. In fact, the master chefs excelled in their talents to such a great extent that they are believed to have received salaries more than that of the Prime Minister himself.

In this period alone, there were more poets than in any other part of the country. Subsequently the Mughal monarchy was battling for its survival and in their sinking empire, had no time for patronizing creative talent. This led to the influx of several artists to Lucknow where they received considerable patronage. Cultural refinement was thus not just confined to the courts but thrived even on the streets and by-lanes of this ancient and historical city.

3

Seat of Fine Arts

Time was (before Independence) when Lucknow was like a sequestered lady behind the veil. Now and again a few novelists and romantists came over to take a peep. Rudyard Kipling was the most famous of this tribe. He called the city 'Nucklow' affectionately which is saying much for Kipling was a hard man to please. For the rest they came and saw and if they were conquered they kept it a secret. Lucknow has now emerged into the limelight, in the words of a poet:-

"O when will the day come; when you will come,

Unveiled and unashamed before the Assembly."

Well the 'day' came with Independence and Lucknow went straight to the Assembly where it is being discussed ever since. Schools, colleges, educational institutions, literary organisations, musical soirees, cultural programmes, museums, auditoriums and stadiums have changed the face of the city and Lucknow has taken its place among the social elite. One good result is that it is witnessing a remarkable cavalcade of visitors, tourists, educationists, research enthusiasts and critics as never before.

Lucknow has its admirers (and critics) in New Hampshire and Iowa and most of the States in the western world, as also in Tomsk and Murmansk and the new pioneer cities in central Siberia. Fulbright tutors, exchange scholars straight from the university campus, scholars from the Ford Foundation, people of every age and interest; experimentalism in International Living, research workers and historians take care that Lucknow does not remain in the backwaters of the world's intellectual life.

Lucknow and literature are closely bracketed. The city is wedded to romances in Urdu, Hindi and English and the Muse has treated Lucknow as a place for fairy tales. In recent times, Lucknow has become the theme for many popular pictures, particularly in Muslim social films. Films have come to have a tremendous effect on the way of life and culture of the people of all classes and glimmerings from the last days of Lucknow have illuminated many a theme which are the "talk of the nation".

Even if the Lucknow culture and way of life are completely defaced, it is sure that one departing from Lucknow will hesitate to board the train before offering to follow 'after you' *tehzeeb*.

The mainstream of Lucknow 's culture is the traditional etiquette and humility of the great towards the small. Democracy is found with a warm welcome here, and the Arts are embraced with passion. Traditions everywhere become the part and parcel of people, and a groove has been carved by the stream of centuries so deep and compelling, that even those traditions, which seem difficult and out-of-date, are observed with reverence.

4

Blend of the Old and the New

Perhaps no other town of recent origin has a more romantic history than the city of Lucknow, the capital of Uttar Pradesh. The mention of its name still conjures up visions of the Nawabs of Avadh and their gorgeous retinue, their luxurious palaces and stately harems, of gaily-clad maidens and dancing girls swaying delicately in unison with the tinkling of tiny bells tied to their feet. These and many such reminiscences plunge the mind into sad moodiness, as one listens to the city's past from some wrinkled mouth acting as a self-appointed guide in the suburbs of Hussainabad.

Picturesque and peaceful, Lucknow is situated on both the sides of the river Gomti which flows across the city. Though Lucknow truly can make no claim to any singular material achievement, its magnanimity of culture reflected in its subtle fusion of sophistication and emotional warmth, its elegant language and the refined manners of its people-all together distinguish it from scores of other small and big cities of India. The Sham-e-Avadh' is second to none in colour and variety. The greatest attraction of Lucknow, however, lies in the art of assimilating the old and the new.

Chhota Imambara

An undying monument of Muslim architecture- built by Mohd. Ali Shah as a burial place for himself and his wife.

The city traces its origin to Lord Lakshman, the brother of Lord Rama, who is said to have founded the town around the spot now called the Lakshman Tila - a sloppy mound near the Hardinge Bridge. Some say that the city owes its name to Lakshman, an aıchitect employed by the Muslim rulers of Jaunpur to build the mediaeval Lucknow. Whatever be the truth, Lucknow really came into prominence during the last quarter of the 18th century when, Asaf-ud-daula made the town his capital, and designed and remodeled Lucknow by constructing edifices like the Roomi Darwaza, the Bara Imambara and the Bibiapur Kothi. During his time Lucknow's fame as the main seat of culture spread far and wide. Poets, philosophers, musicians and beautiful courtesans flocked to the court of the Nawab and Lucknow outshone even the Imperial Court at Delhi. Tired of the inhospitality and coldness of Delhi, celebrities like Ghalib and Mir fled to the climate of Lucknow where they were warmly received by the Nawabs.

Lucknow's fall was no less dramatic than its rise. During the reign of Wajid Ali Shah, the city reached the peak of its degenerated glory. In 1856, the British annexed the Kingdom of Oudh and the following year India's First War of Independence was waged. It was a period of bitter trials and tribulations. Pitched battles were fought in streets and parks everywhere and battered walls, half-razed buildings and ruins scattered all over the city remind one even today of that grim and tumultuous period of our history.

Later, the British made Lucknow the *de facto* capital of the State and with the establishment of Government offices, military cantonment and expansion and development of educational and other institutions, the city grew rapidly and regained much of its lost glory.

Tomb Of Saadat Ali Khan

It is one of the many imposing constructions of the Nawabi period.

Central Sports Stadium known as K.D. Singh Babu Stadium

Lucknow presents a wide and variegated spectacle to any newcomer. Time's ravages have wrought no havoc to the old Lucknow as most of its important buildings were constructed either towards the close of the 18th century or afterwards. Even today the Government House, the Museum, the Roshan-ud-daula kachehri and many schools and laboratories are located in buildings which belonged to the Nawabs. In the heart of the city itself, people live in their old ancestral homes, many of which have a story to tell.

Lucknow's architecture is borrowed from too many styles but in its entirety rich and extravagantly distinct.

In the oldest part of the city is the Bara Imambara built by Nawab Asaf-ud-daula in 1784. According to a legend, it was constructed to provide relief to the people from a terrible famine. Men and veiled women from respectable families worked on it at nights to earn their living and the generous Nawab prolonged its construction till the ordeal was over. A flight of steps lead to a platform on which stands a magnificent hall said to be the largest in the world. A unique feature of the hall is that no pillars support the ceiling of this massive structure. Roomi Darwaza, Hussainabad Clock Tower, Picture Gallery, the Chhota Imambara, Juma Masjid and Lakshman-ka-Tila constitute the main group of historical buildings in the Hussainabad area. During the Moharram thousands of persons visit the Imambaras to witness the grand illumination.

Among the important historical monuments in the city, the Lucknow Residency stands a little away from the frontal bank of the Gomti where the bullet-ridden structure and broken column narrate their story.

A little east to the Residency is the tall Chhatar Manzil overlooking the Gomti with a beautiful dome surrounded with a golden umbrella, which has given it its present name. The buildings at present house the Central Drug Research Institute.

The Tomb of Saadat Ali Khan, the Khursheed Manzil, Shah Najaf, Kaiserbagh and Baradari are among the other principal constructions of the Nawabi period.

Not less famous on account of its gardens and parks, Lucknow has aptly been called the City of Gardens. Reminiscent of the olden days, Sikandar Bagh, Banarasi Bagh and Dilkusha still have enough to charm the visitors. Across the Gomti where the tall-domed buildings of Lucknow University stand, once stood the magnificent Badshahbagh, but today only a red-stone Baradari and a small bridge across an artificial lake opposite the Tagore Library serve as momentous.

Amid a host of educational institutions in the town, Isabella Thoburn College, Lucknow University, Medical College, Palaeobotanic Institute, J.K. Institute of Sociology, Central Drug Research Institute and the Nadawatul Ulema (The Arabic College) are the most prominent. The Government College of Arts and Crafts imparts training to artists in drawing, painting, sculpture and commercial art while the Bhatkhande University of Indian Music, founded in 1926, is a famous place for Hindustani music and dances, where students from countries like Ceylon, Burma and the Middle East come to learn melodies of Indian music.

The U.P. Government's Handicraft Emporium is open everyday excepting on Sundays and Government holidays from 10 a.m. to 8 p.m. On display at the Emporium are the largest selection of the State's arts and crafts, various brocades and silks, Lucknow and Agra embroidery, Almora Woollens, Farrukhabad prints, Mirzapur carpets, Khurja pottery and Moradabad brassware.

Kashmir Emporium : On display at the Emporium are a variety of Kashmir products, shawls, silks, peppier mashie, furs, wood carvings, carpets, honey and saffron.

Gandhi Ashram : For sale here are hand spun and hand-woven clothes called 'Khadi', closely associated with our freedom struggle, coloured Indian prints, silks, rough woollen materials and leather goods. Here, one may buy literature on and by Mahatma Gandhi.

Aminabad: One of the arteries from Hazratganj passes through Kaiserbagh to Aminabad, which is the busiest part of the city. Within its thronging enclosure is the market where one can buy almost anything particularly in the evenings when Aminabad glitters with lights. The fruit-stalls are full with delicious 'lichis' (in season) which is a speciality of Lucknow. The 'Lungra' mangoes are another speciality, and watermelons too. In Aminabad there are also the old 'Kulfi' shops, the '*sharbat*' stalls and the flower vendors. Here one can buy '*Itr*' too, the old perfumes and distilled essences which should be sparingly used. The most famous of these is the '*Khus*' made out of a special grass, and the remarkable 'Itr' which exudes the perfume of moist wet earth. In Aminabad one can buy the unique Lucknow 'Zari' of gold and silver threads which makes a gorgeous gift, spiced tobacco, betel leaves and beetle-nuts, silver-embroidered silks and glass bangles.

Chowk: Every old city in India has a locality called the 'Chowk'. The most famous is the 'Chandni Chowk' of Delhi, Hyderabad in Andhra Pradesh has its Chowk, and for that matter Lucknow too. The Lucknow Chowk is a narrow lane bracketed between two gates and is the fountain head of its music and arts. Some of the oldest families, who had escaped the aftermath of the 1857 War of Independence still live there. It is the centre of Lucknow jewelry work, its silver wares and its famous 'chikan' work. The street is so narrow that cars are not permitted to enter from 6 p.m. to 9 p.m. The Chowk is closed on Thursday but open on Sundays.

Nakhas: Close to the Chowk is Nakhas where every Sunday a weekly market is held and purchases can be made at bargain prices provided the customer has ample reserves of patience and wit and good humour. If he is a curio collector, he is likely to make a starting addition to his collection.

Lucknow Cuisine: A cruise of Lucknow will not be complete without sampling its cuisine, for Lucknow is the very representative of the State of which it is the capital. Every city in U.P. is well-known for at least one distinctive feature which makes it unique. Allahabad, the old Prayag, is the venue of the oldest and the greatest Mela in India. Agra has its Taj, Kanpur its factories, Nainital its lake and Terai and Lucknow its Imambaras, handicrafts, traditions and delicacies.

If you are fortunate enough to have your own : I kitchen then look around for a good Lucknow cook. He may be a cheat, but he knows his job well. While your loose change disappear into thin air, your gastronomic demands will be soothed and satisfied with aromatic delicacies such as Biryani, Murgh Musallam, various kinds of Korma, Keema, Koftas and Kababs. Lucknow, being a city situated on the banks of the Gomti on which fishermen ply their ancient trade, is famous for fish preparations. But fish, though popular, is by no means

Bara Imambara (Moharram Illuminations)

This magnificent building was constructed by Asaf-ud-daula in 1784 to provide relief to the poor from a terrible famine.

plentiful and purchases should be made early in the mornings to avoid disappointments. Lucknow is also famous for its sweets, made from a special preparation of cream called *balai*. Melons and mangoes are plentiful in summer. Mahliabad is full of different varieties of Mangoes.

5

Tourist Spots

Lucknow never takes the first place either as a city or as a tourist attraction. But doubtless it occupies an imposing ‘second’ in almost every aspect of Indian cultural life, history, art, music, education etc. This gives it a variety of faces. The attractive, the inviting, the unique and the impossible glare at each other and the passerby from every square and corner of the city. The visitor will do well to begin with the old buildings of Lucknow. These are not old enough to be antique although they may be antiquated.

The Bara Imambara - Imambara is a place where the Moharram is observed. Lucknow has some notable ones. The most well-known and impressive is the Bara Imambara built by Nawab Asaf-ud-daulah in 1784, to provide works and relief to the poor when famine stalked through Avadh. The way to it is over a gateway to the main gateway which opens on a big quadrangle. To the right over a flight of steps stands the great Mosque. Immediately in the front is the Imambara. The building is of vast proportions and the main hall is thought to be one of the largest of its kind in the world- 63 ft. long, 53 ft. high and 53 ft. wide. Its unique feature is the labyrinth

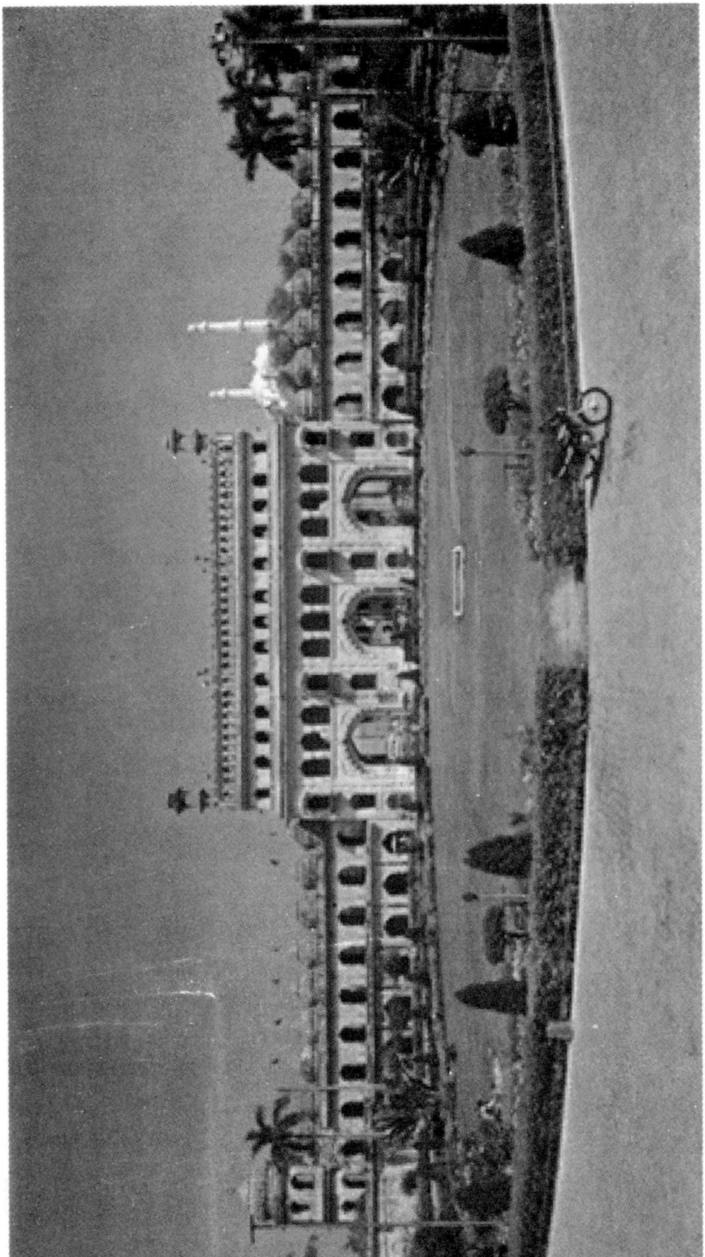

A View of Bara Imambara revealing the complex and rich architecture of the Nawabi Era

Chota Imambara

An octagonal tank with a drawbridge leads to the entrance at the lmambara which is *mounted with a white dome.*

bhool bhulaiya which is the only one of its kind in the country. A maze of corridors, causeway and arches in which the newcomer gets quickly lost, and it is difficult to find one's way out without a guide. Visitors are always accompanied by a guide whose service could be hired for a small fee. Close to the Bara Imambara is the Roomi Darwaza, a solitary gateway with ornamental designs radiating from the base to the turret. The Arch is 60 ft. high.

The Picture Gallery and the Hussainabad Clock Tower - Erected by Mohammad Ali Shah, the Hussainabad Clock Tower rises 221 ft. high. At the foot of the tower is a large octagonal tank. The tower and tank were built in 1831.

A double storey red-brick building houses life size portraits of the rulers of Avadh and is called the picture gallery. It was built by Mohammad Ali Shah.

Hussainabad Imambara - also called the Chhota Imambara : was built by Mohammad Ali Shah in

Lucknow University.

1837, as a burial place for himself and his wife. The building is very ornate and stands in a big garden. An octagonal tank with a drawbridge leads to the entrance of the Imambara which is mounted with a white dome.

The interior is adorned with gilt edged mirrors, stucco of varied colours, chandeliers and Tazias. With the first step inside, the visitor is taken a hundred years back, the aura of the feudal past clings heavily to the walls and the furniture, and the atmosphere is laden with moth, dust and bat-wing.

The Juma Masjid - or the Friday Mosque is situated south-west of the Chhota Imambara. It is built on an enormous scale. Though begun by Mohammad Ali Shah, it was completed by Begum Malika Jehan.

Kaiser Bagh - Once the 'harem' of the last ruler Avadh, Wajid Ali Shah, Kaiser Bagh is a magnificent quadrangle surrounded by yellow buildings, girdled by a ring of groves and parks. Many of its spacious edifices now house Modern institutions. In the centre is a stone building called the 'Baradari' surrounded on all sides by large parks and courts with marble pavilions. One of the buildings to the east is occupied by the Bhatkhande University of Indian Music, and the archaeological section of the State Museum. On the west is another impressive structure which houses the Amiruddaulla Public Library.

Khurshed Manzil- Situated near the State Bank, it was intended as a resting-place for the mother of Ghaziuddin Haider, who completed it. It has a marked European appearance after the fashion set by the Frenchman Martin and is designed like a mediaeval European castle with towers and moats. Today it houses the La Martiniere School for Girls.

The Begum Kothi - The Begum Kothi was, called, the Old Post Office in Hazratganj. It was built in 1844 by King Amjad Ali Shah for his queen Malka Ahad Begum. The building played a significant role towards the end of the Mutiny when in March, 1858 it was lost to the English after a severe battle.

Shah Najaf - A big white-domed building close to the Girl's La Martiniere is the tomb of Nawab Ghaziuddin Haider (1814-1827) and his favorite wife. The interior is decorated with chandeliers and floral designs and the tombs are of solid silver and gold.

La Martiniere College for Boys - On the eastern outskirts of the city near the military cantonment, is the famous palace designed by General Claude Martin and completed in 1795. Martin was a fabulous figure who came to India to try his luck with the French East India Company and rose to be a trusted General in the British army. He did well in business also. He left the bulk of his enormous fortune for founding three schools at Lucknow, Calcutta and his native city of Lyons. The visitor will find the architecture of the building, which has gargoyles and Corinthian Capitals, Roman arches and oriental terraces, somewhat bewildering. The extensive grounds and the school chapel are worth exploring. The school derives its name from its motto, "Labour et Constantia."

Lucknow Zoo - Lucknow is proud of its open-air zoological garden. The Prince of Wales Zoological Garden, in which tigers and lions are allowed to roam about in specially, designed cages to resemble their natural habitation. There are many prize specimens in the Zoo, including a rhinoceros from Assam, panthers, elephants and monkeys.

6

The Barrage at the Residency: 1857

A year after the deposition of Wajid Ali Shah, many of the palaces, so extravagantly erected, were cannonaded down and the piles of rubble were splattered with blood. All over Northern India, the soldiers employed by the British East India Company were rebelling against their foreign employers. In Lucknow the struggle was fierce and unhappy for both sides. The European population took refuge in the British Residency Compound where for five months they were besieged by the sepoy rebels, who held all the other important buildings.

It was on May 30, 1857 that the siege began. Sir Henry Lawrence and his advisors were sitting quietly over a glass of wine. They had stored provisions - the badminton court was piled to the ceiling with fodder; the cellar was filled with flour. They had barricaded and walled and dug. They waited.

There were 3,000 members of the compound to start with, 927 British officers, private and civilians and

The bullet ridden Structure and the broken Columns of Residency narrate the Story of the Struggle for Independence.

700 loyal sepoys. These were the defenders of 700 coolies and 600 women and children.

On the 29th of June the fighting force was reduced to 293 at the Battle of Chinhat. Misled by the false intelligence reports, Sir Henry Lawrence led 600 men on a reconnaissance mission. He thought the opposing force to be 500 on foot, 500 horses and one gun, but it was a polished, artilleries force of 6000 which met them and surprised the British troops who had rounded a corner on the Chinhat Road.

As Lawrence's men straggled back to the stronghold, five guns and 293 men were left behind. Seventy-eight of those who returned were sick or wounded and took their places on the floor of the banquet hall-turned hospital. Medicine in those days could do little for them and often made things worse with ignorance about infections. With the loss of these men, Lawrence could no longer support a garrison at the Old Macchi Bhawan Fort, one mile up the river. Some of its wall represented the earliest settlements of the area, but now it contained barrels of gun powder had ammunition and so had to be blown up.

July 2, 8.00 hrs, four days after Chinhat, the weary Henry Lawrence climbed up to his apartment in the Residency. Everyone looked to him for leadership and, though he had been ill, his working hours were long. He lay down on his bed and began discussing ration distribution with his aide-camp. Suddenly there was a great clap in the air, a yellow flash and bricks showered from the ceiling. The aid called out to his leader. The answer came back painfully, "I am killed." A cannonball had ripped away Lawrence's thigh and pelvis. The Resident lived three days more, dictating instructions and his own epitaph, "Here lies Henry Lawrence who tried to do his duty".

Morale took a plunge, Scurvy from lack of fresh fruit and vegetables began to take its toll. Wounds did not heal and internal hemorrhages appeared. Rations were cut, the besieged held out only with the hope that General Henry Havelock would come through Kanpur and provide relief.

But Havelock's column was much beleaguered elsewhere and unable to reach Lucknow until September 25, the 88th day of the siege. When it did arrive, it was not a relieving force, but a starving, exhausted bunch that only swelled the ranks. They had come through the centre of Lucknow and had been fired upon from the buildings. Of the 2000 who had made it to Lucknow, 535 became causalities a few yards from the Balley Guard Gate in front of the Residency. Many wounded crowded into the hospital to fight it out with death there. Now the one hope of the British in Lucknow was to hold out until new forces arriving from England could work up country from Calcutta for the final rescue.

Food rations shrank and clothes became quite old, but there were a few who managed to carry on with fairly good humour. When a surgeon prescribed a change of diet for a lady with blotches and sores, she said, "I wonder you don't prescribe a change of air." November 10, Henry Kavanagh, a red headed Irishman disguised as a native was able to sneak from the Residency through the outskirts of the town, made his way past Alam Bagh and eighteen miles out of Lucknow to where Sir Colin Campbell and his forces had gathered for the second rescue attempt. There, he presented a plan of the city from which Campbell could form a plan of rescue for the others.

First the force would march to Alam Bagh where an advanced guard was in semaphore communication with the Residency. Tents and heavy baggage were to be left there. Next a sweep round the city would take them through Dilkusha Park, past La Martiniere College and through Sikandra Bagh, east of the Residency. One by one these had to be captured from the large forces of rebel sepoys and then held while main column made its advance to the rescue.

On November 16, the advance was made. Dilkusha was ruined with cannon; La Martiniere was taken easily as it was deserted; 1857 were slaughtered at Sikandra Bagh. Then there remained one strong rebel post between Sir Colin Campbell and the Residency which was Shah Najaf, and he managed to occupy that the same night. The total number of casualties had been 43 officers, 450 men killed or wounded on the British side and an unknown number of rebel sepoys.

Kavanagh, the Irishman, was able to effect a meeting between leaders of the two parties, rescuers and to-be-rescued. The secret plans for evacuation from the Residency at night were made.

November 1922 : The Naval Artillery directed a barrage on Kaiser Bagh, a rebel centre, to divert attention from the exodus. In some places along the routes, canvas screens were propped up as camouflage. In others, the way was made through trenches. The ground captured by Campbell's troops was retraced, building by building, first by women, children and wounded, then by the old garrison and Havelock's men and, finally, Campbell's men joined behind and followed through Sikandra Bagh to Alam Bagh. The relief of Lucknow was completed.

7

La Martiniere College

Dilkusha : This garden is near the Boys' Martiniere. Originally the Nawabs' hunting lodge, it was severely damaged during the war of 1857. The ruins, eucalyptus groves and a well-planned garden make it a popular picnic spot.

Government College of Arts and Crafts. Adjoining the University is the State-aided Arts school. With Mr Ashit Haldar as Principal, the Institution achieved national importance and attracted artists from all over the land. Students learn drawing, painting and sculpture as well as pottery making and metal work in the school. A section in the school assists the Government in improving cottage industries.

Chowk: This is the oldest and was, once the most famous market of Lucknow. Today it is a narrow lane with two gates at either end. Built by the Mughal Emperors, Akbar and Jehangir, at one time, it used to be the centre of art and music, for the famous courtesans who used to

La Martiniere College

have their salons in the neighbourhood and the feudal aristocracy made it their favourite haunt. The oldest families of the city still live in its alleys and the core of Nawabi manners persists among the dwellers of the Chowk.

On either side of the narrow lane are artilleries where artisans make all kinds of things from beaten silver to fancy Hubble-bubbles. The retail merchants are often themselves entrepreneurs. Since the street is narrow, cars are not allowed to enter it after 6 p.m. The best time for shopping is early evening.

The Chowk is the best place for buying Lucknow Handicrafts, the most famous being Chiken-white embroidery work generally done on white cotton. The designs and motifs follow traditional patterns-mango, leaf, elephant and fish. One can buy almost anything from embroidered, sarees and blouse-pieces to shirts, table linen and children's clothes. Silver and gold

Council House- Where the Two Houses of Legislature Meet.

Hazrat Ganj - Market 1958

embroidery, another specialty of Lucknow, is generally not done on readymade garments, but scarves and borders are available. Lucknow now specializes in heavy silver jewelry such as thick necklaces, anklets and earrings. Both Aminabad and Chowk are closed on Thursday but open on Sundays.

The Chhatar Manzil : is located some distance away from the Residency. Its interior is magnificently decorated and furnished. Its halls and rooms are spacious and handsome. For some time it served as a palace for Begum Hazrat Mahal, the heroine of India's first fight for independence, who resided there during the struggle. The palace today houses the Central Drug Research Institute.

The Mausoleums : Overlooking the Chhatar Manzil and facing the centre of the city are the two mausoleums built by Ghaziuddin Haider for Nawab Saadat Ali Khan and his beautiful Wife Khursheed Begum. The domes of the tombs are the best in Lucknow.

Aurangzeb's Mosque: In old Lucknow is situated a majestic mosque built by the Emperor Aurangzeb. The high ground on which it stands, is called Lakshman Ka Tila, and is of great antiquity. Lucknow is said to be named, after Lakshman, who founded the city in the hoary past.

Moti Mahal: It was constructed by Nawab Saadat-Ali-Khan between 1798 and 1814. It was from Mobarak Manzil within the same compound that the King used to watch the fights of large animals. The campus now has a good library-Acharya Narendra Dev library which caters to the needs of the University students'. The Library is maintained by the Moti Lal Nehru Memorial Society, which runs many other educational and child-welfare institutions. The Moti Mahal is surrounded by beautiful gardens and mango groves. It was at Moti Mahal that in

BARADARI, Kaiser Bagh

This beautiful monument was once the part of palace and has some piece of French Statuary

1857 the relieving forces led by Sir James Outram and Sir Henry Havelock joined hands with the local British forces. This was the turning point for Lucknow and its fight for independence. There are two stones in and just outside the Moti Mahal commemorating this union of the relieved and the relieving forces on 17th November, 1857.

The Lal Baradari : The Lal Baradari was built by Nawab Saadat Ali Khan- between 1789 and 1814. The building stands opposite the Great Chhatar Manzil. It was built as the Coronation Hall and Royal Durbar. The building is painted brick-red and hence the name.

The building is now used for art exhibitions, called Lalit Kala Akademi.

During the reign of Nasir-ud-din Haider many changes were made in the interior decoration of the Lal Baradari. During his reign, one William Knighton visited the Baradari and described it as "Lavishly decorated with scarlet and gold tapestry. Dim light filtered through the windows enchanting the solemnity of the royal receptions. The throne was of great value and consisted of a platform approached by six steps. Three sides were of solid silver richly ornamented with jewels. Former kings had been content to sit in oriental fashion upon a velvet cushion placed on this platform; but Nasir-ud-din was too westernized and insisted on having gold "on ivory chair."

8

Groves, Gardens and Parks

Lucknow can justly claim the title of City of Gardens. The Sikandar Bagh, laid out by the last Nawab, is now the National Botanical Gardens. The Banarsi Bagh, with its Zoological Gardens, is a pride of the city. The Dilkusha, originally a hunting lodge for the Nawabs, is now a popular picnic spot. Badshah Bagh, where the impressive buildings of the University-situated was once a beautiful laid-out garden; a discarded Hammam (bath) and a Baradari (open pavilion), are all that remain of it now. Besides the larger gardens and parks, Lucknow abounds in lovely avenues of shady trees, green groves and well maintained little public and private gardens.

Martyrs' Memorial: In the centenary year of 1957 was put up this noble memorial, almost opposite the Residency, on the banks of the Gomati. A tall, stately column, unadorned and unyielding, stands in the midst of a small but well maintained part in memory of those who lost their lives in the memorable struggle.

Butler Palace

Built in the English regime this magnificent building combines in it Nawabi as well as English architecture.

Sikandar Bagh : This was originally planned by the last of the Nawabs for his favorite wife, in whose honour it was named. It was completely devastated in 1857.

What now remain are parts of the eastern wall and beautiful gateway, rebuilt in 1903. The British developed it into a provincial horticultural garden. In 1953, Council of Scientific and Industrial Research took it over for development as the first National Botanical Garden of India. Its herbarium, fern-houses, nurseries as well as its excellent facilities for research attract experts from all over the world. To the casual observer its smooth lawns, shady trees and flower-beds are a welcome retreat.

Lawns and Parks: There are many little patches of lawns and flowers here and there, notable among them, on account of the number of visitors they draw, is the one at the foot of the Monkey Bridge, and the other at the foot of the Martyrs's Memorial on the right bank of the Gomati opposite the Residency.

9

Principal Institutions

Lucknow University: The royal gardens of the Walis have disappeared, but in its place has risen the University of Lucknow, Canning College was founded in 1864, and acquired the estate in 1905 which is now the University campus. The University of Lucknow has five Faculties those of Arts, Science, Commerce, Law and Medicine. It has many libraries, but the biggest is the Tagore Library consisting of 1,25,000 books. The Library also houses a museum and an art gallery.

The King George Medical College is situated near the Bara lmambara, and its exquisite gardens are worth a visit.

Birbal Sahani Institute of Palaeobotany contains rare specimens of flora fossils. The institute is named after the famed botanist, Dr. Birbal Sahani who died in 1949.

Central Drug Research Institute is housed in the Chhatar Manzil, once the palace of Begum Hazrat Mahal. The institute is one of the chains of twelve national laboratories formed in the country since

King George's Medical College

Its Hospital section is known as Gandhi Memorial and Associated Hospitals

Isabella Thoburn College

Independence. The purpose of this institute is to test and standardize drugs.

Isabella Thoburn College was founded by Miss Isabella Thoburn, an American Methodist Missionary, in 1870. In the beginning it was only a school for girls but was later raised to the status of a college in 1886, and was subsequently affiliated to Lucknow University. The Isabella Thoburn College is easily one of the premier institutions of learning for women in India.

Nadwatul Ulema is housed in an old majestic building in the old city. The institution is one of the renowned centres of Arabic learning in India. It was founded in 1890.

Bhatkhande University of Indian Music: Founded by the renowned musician Vishnu Digamber Bhatkhande in 1926, the institution has rendered great service in revitalizing Indian music, particularly the North Indian modes of musical style in vocal and instrumental music and also dances. It is the only one of its kind in the country.

Government College of Fine Arts and Crafts: Trains aspiring young men and women with artistic aptitudes in drawing, painting, sculpture. and commercial art. It has already produced some eminent artists.

The State Museum: The Museum is open all days from 10 a.m. to 4 p.m. except on Wednesday. It is worth paying a visit, for in many ways it is unique. The museum has four main divisions, archaeological, anthropological, natural history and art. The coin and art sections have specimens ranging from coins of the Kushan period to that of the Rajput, Mughal, and Deccani periods.

Soochna Kendra is the State's Information Centre. It has a Library-cum-Reading Room, an excellent

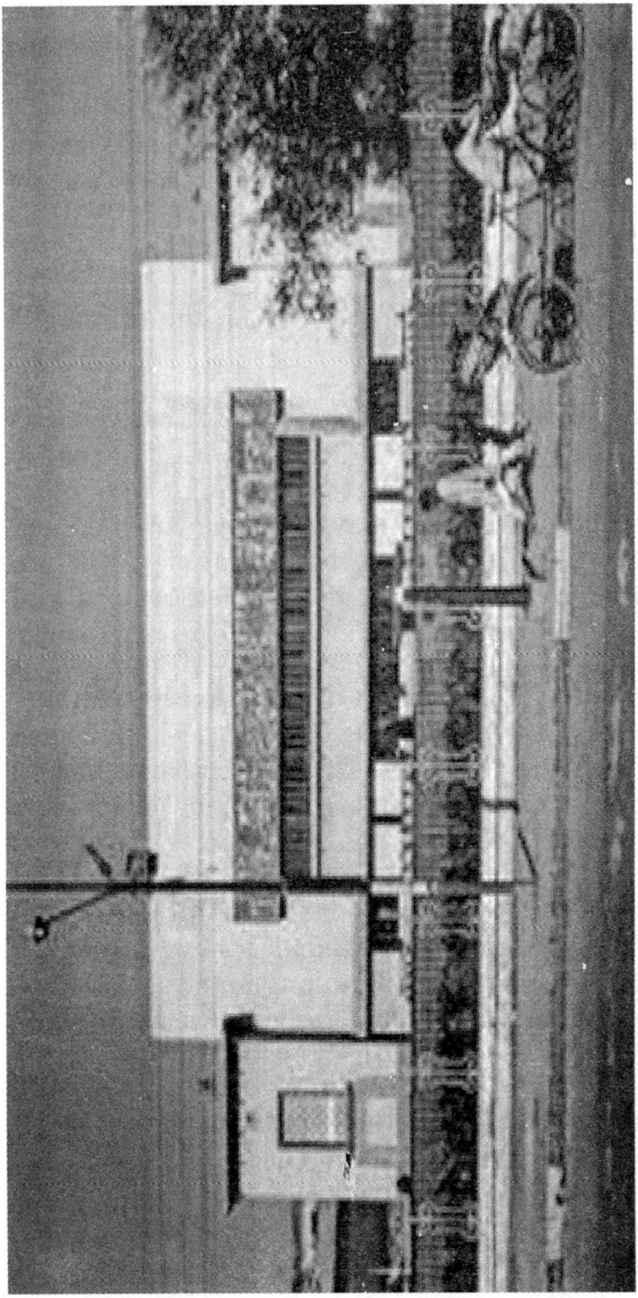

Ravindralaya

The aesthetic look of the building- its elegance and simplicity- is very much in keeping with the poet's great ideals. It has also an up-to-date and well-equipped auditorium.

Reference Library and Women's and Children's section. It screens films for women and children once a week.

Rabindra Kendra: is a fitting memorial to the great poet, Rabindranath Tagore. The aesthetic look of the building- its elegance and simplicity- is in keeping with the poet's great ideals. It contains literature on Tagore and his works.

Bakshi-ka-Talab : is a centre for the training of development personnel.

Road Research Institute : This is an organisation of the Uttar Pradesh Government Research programmes directed towards the achievement of economy and efficiency in the design, construction and maintenance of roads are being tackled by this institution. Dissemination of research results and guidance to highway departments are it principal aims.

Railway Testing and Research Centre: Established in 1952 and has even since been under the aegis of the Railway Board, Government of India. Its research programme concerns branches of engineering and such aspects as fuels, dynamic effects of vehicles on track and bridges, riding quality, performance of locomotives, rolling stock assemblies and components. It has added to the status of Indian Railways which is the biggest nationalized undertaking in the country and the second largest individual railway network in the world.

Government Precision Instruments Factory : This new Uttar Pradesh Government factory makes many kinds of precision instruments and meter and is a very successful venture in a new field of manufacture in the country.

Mahanagar Township : This is a neighbourhood township, developed by the Uttar Pradesh Government through the local Municipal Board or Nagar Nigam. It is a fine example of modern town planning and the way to tackle the housing problem under the present day conditions.

10

Entertaining

Lucknow entertains its guests with obvious pleasure, savouring every moment of it. Though extravagant, entertaining is not done much any more, anyone from the East, West or South can immediately feel the difference in atmosphere in a typical Lucknow home. This is perhaps because of the Nawabi legacy.

In the days of the Nawabs, a host tried to see that his party would be talked about for days afterwards and there was tremendous competition to provide the most delightful meals and after dinner entertainment. Singers and dancers were invariably hired for the night. The guest's pleasure was the host's pleasure.

It is said that a famous nawab became tired of serving the same dishes every time he had a party. He rocked his brain to find some novel way of serving food and hit upon an idea. When the guests were seated they were served with kababs and parathas. When they broke into the kababs, live quail flew out from each one. The guests were surprised and applauded their host who, needless to say, felt quite smug!

Though, the fashion presently tends towards simpler entertainment, there are some who continue to provide qawwali singers for special occasions. And even today, some professional cooks use great subtlety in preparing dishes. They often camouflage certain kinds of food so that guests do not know what exactly they are eating.

A Lucknowite should never be hurried through his meal. He likes to take his time. Though he is used to eating well, one need not think that he expects to see hundreds of dishes on the table. He liked variety, yes, but more than that he likes a well planned, well prepared meal.

When planning a dinner party whether it be for six or twenty people, rotis (Indian bread) must be served. Pullao is served if the dessert is something other than zarda (sweet rice), but Lucknow people are not all that fond of rice. At the usual dinner one finds both parathas and plain rotis (one with ghee and the other dry). Kababs are a must with parathas and when guests are seated at a table, this combination is served first. Rice is never served first, as it may be construed as a tactless effort on the part of the hostess to get her guest to eat less. Of course, for a buffet dinner, all the dishes are arranged together on a table and the guests help themselves. In addition to the meat and rotis there should be at least two green vegetables, salad and a yogurt preparation.

A good hostess will make it a point to know before hand which guests are vegetarian guests, it is best to have a meatless *pullao* and a curried vegetable like *mattor paneer* in addition to other dishes. Pea Pullao or dried fruit pullao may be substituted for *pullao* and *qorma*. Also a fresh salad should be without onions as some vegetarians don't eat onions.

A decorative meal is always appetizing. Fresh mint and coriander leaves are invariably used generously. Silver leaves are used for halwas and other sweets. A variety of pickles whether the guests eat them or not, are kept on the table. After dinner, pan is served on a silver tray with a variety of betel nuts, aniseed or special mixture called *gota*. A few people like to take a little tobacco covered with silver leaf. Pan is very essential part of a menu. Maghai pan plain or with peppermint is very popular.

11

The Maharaj Family of Kathak Dances

Prasad, as dance teacher to Nawab Wajid Ali Shah, established one of the first schools for the Kathak Dance. Under court patronage he was able to develop his own style and transmit it to his sons as the modern Kathak Dance.

His sons, Binda Din and Kalka, were his chief pupils. Kalka is said to have been light hearted, a colourful Bohemian, a popular hero who played the tabla with verve for his brother. Binda Din is more famous as a dancer. It is said that he perfected the three main aspects of the dance, namely, Nrittia in which all the movements of the body combine with the intricate rhythms of the feet; Gats in which the gestures, movements and facial expressions reveal the story of Lord Krishna's life; and Abhinaya, a creative dramatization of words or sentiments completely dependent on the inventive skills of the artist. It was Binda Din and Lachhu Maharaj who made notations on these skills for future and Lachhu Maharaj.

Binda Din's keenest student was his nephew Achchan Maharaj who has never been surpassed they say in creative, improvisational footwork. His frenzied but perfect foot-rhythms made his audience forget to breathe.

Achchan Maharaj passed the torch to his younger brothers Lachoo and Shambhoo Maharaj and to Brij Mohan, all of whom became masters of the art. As a young boy, Shambhoo Maharaj danced wonderfully at the All-India Music Conference held in Lucknow in 1926. As the years passed he became widely known as one of the greatest living exponents of the art and received an Akademi Award in recognition of his contribution to the classical arts of India. Living legend is Lachoo Maharaj.

12

Lucknow by Night

In old Lucknow, there was a regular provision for night life at various points particularly in the eastern wing of the city. The Nawabi Era witnessed in abundance a host of social-cultural activities in the form of frequent Mushairas, Mujrahs, classical music and dance recitals. Some of these presentations were a regular feature in several areas of the city. Society upheld all artistic and aesthetic values that mattered in those good old days; and while the law provided for their full play, the aristocracy extended to them the fullest patronage and protection.

But now, however the aura of night life has undergone some changes, and a few quarters of the city buzz with the goings-on of nightly entertainment programmes. Among the hotels that cater to the demands of night diversion are Hotel Clarks Avadh and Carlton Hotel. At the former, which is the only five star hotel of the city, there is ample provision for regular entertainment. Divided into several sections, Clarks Avadh has a bar-cum-restaurant named 'Gulfam' on its ground floor. It is a beauteous resort and in a sense rendezvous for the easing of one's tension and strained nerves after the mundane day-to-day activities, by reason of its placid atmosphere.

Tourists find 'Gulfam' in Hotel Clarks Avadh well worth a visit for a recess and respite from the noise and din of sight-seeing and other engagements. On the 9th floor of the majestic hotel which overlooks the Gomati flinted by the Lucknow University buildings, is the famed 'Dragon' where there is a regular cabaret and other music programmes in the evening. One specialty of the 'Dragon' is that apart from other choice dishes it serves Chinese preparations in a sizeable variety. This is indeed exquisite apartment of the hotel, calculated in every sense to captivate visitors with its aesthetic layout and aura in general.

Apart from the hotels there are the clubs where cards, music, billiards, swimming and tennis and other forms of entertainment are to be found. There is the Mohammad Bagh Club, the Gymkhana Club, Jenisis Club and the Lucknow Club, to name only the more popular ones. While each one of them has its own attractions and ways and means of recreation all contribute in some degree or other to night life in the city. At the Mohammad Bagh Club, there are special music items or Ball Room Dance almost every month for the entertainment of members and guests. May Queen Ball, September Queen and New Year Eve dance are very popular. The Lucknow club, Gymkhana Club, and the Mohammad bagh Club have their own billiards-saloons and card-playing arrangements.

13

Sangeet Natya Bharati

India has three unique treasures which she must cherish and protect. Her forests and Wild Life, her Monuments and her Music.

It must be confessed at the outset that like our monuments our music also is greatly indebted to Muslim influence. It is to Islamic people that we owe the musical nuances which make our music so appealing, so compelling.

The Flute, the Veena, and the Sitar, are ancient instruments, but the Sarod, the Sarangi the Esraj, the Dilruba, and the Shehnai are all Muslim Innovations. The lilt and power as in Darbari Kanhara, Asawari Kafi, Yaman, Kalyan, Bhupali, Bhim Palasi, Bageshri and Pilu and many other Ragas and Raginis are mostly due to Muslim influence. They have made our music richer and more vital.

It is a fact that in the past music was encouraged mostly by Muslim rulers. Indeed, some of the names of the Ragas were given to them by Akbar and the later kings. Only Aurangzeb withdrew this patronage. But the Muse continued to be encouraged in some form or other by all the rulers, until with the decline of the Mughal Empire, music deserted the halls of the elect and took its abode in the houses of courtesans and harlots.

They further deteriorated the quality of music in an attempt to preserve the art exclusively among their kinds. The result was a music that lacked refinement and restraint.

It was in this period of extravagance and chaos that efforts were made to establish a college of music in Lucknow. A resolution was passed in the All-India Musical Conference held here in December 1924, in which most of the 'Ustads' and 'Charans' of North India participated.

In the early part of 1926, the All-India College of Hindustani Music was established at Lucknow and named after Sir William Marris the then Governor of Uttar Pradesh.

The Marris College has given a lead in the revival of Hindustani Music and should be looked upon as a major centre of musical instruction and learning in Northern India. Pandit Vishnu Narain Bhatkhande who drew up the curriculum of the college and was the greatest music scholar at that time, came to Lucknow to deliver regular lectures at this institutions. He prescribed a notation system, prepared several textbooks and advised on all technical matters connected with the teaching of music till 1933. In memory of this great savant, the name of Marris College was changed to "Bhatkhande College of Hindustani Music."

In 1926, when this college was started, it had only seven members on the teaching staff and thirteen students, who used one Tanpura, one Sitar and one pair of Tabla.

In 1954, the administration of the College was taken over by the State Government for converting it into a State Academy of Hindustani Music, Dance and Drama. The Uttar Pradesh Sangeet Natya Bharati was established in November, 1963, with the Bhatkhande College of Hindustani Music as its constituent college.

The Akademi is an autonomous body registered under the Act for the registration of literary, scientific and charitable societies. The aims of the Akademi are to co-ordinate and develop the arts of music, dance and drama in the State of Uttar Pradesh and to establish institutions for providing training in music, dance and drama in different centres of U.P., to prescribe standards of education in these fields in the State and to grant degrees and diplomas after regular examinations.

The establishment of the Sangeet Bharati marks a new and promising stage in the development and co-ordination of the art of music, dance and drama in Northern India. For the first time, an institution has been set up for the promotion of dramatics and ballet, including instruction in actor's training, stagecraft and production of plays.

A National Theater has been a long- felt need in Uttar Pradesh. The popular theater everywhere plays an important role in national awakening. In Maharashtra, Madras and Bengal, the drama has molded the thoughts, feelings and aspirations of the common people to an extent hardly experienced in Northern India. All literary men and playwrights should help the Sangeet Bharati to promote the writing and staging of dramas and ballets.

It is essential for national and emotional integration that the teaching of the Hindustani schools of music and dance should be supplemented with instruction in Karnatic music, Bharata Natyam, Manipuri and Kathakali dances. The interpretation of the rich styles of music, song and dance from different music regions of India cannot only powerfully contribute towards like-mindedness but also bring about new creative patterns and movements in music.

Classical music must come to more intimate terms with the far-reaching changes of the Indian landscape and the moods and emotions of Indian mind in the cycle of the seasons. The prevalent classification in music as between high-brow and folk should be mitigated.

High music, like high art and poetry, stimulates the imagination and institution of the people and makes the human soul more responsive to the larger rhythms of life, mind and the universe.

14

Cultural Synthesis

Origin of Name

No authentic earlier history of Lucknow is known: tradition, however, ascribes to it an ancient origin. The legend goes that Lakshmana, brother of Ram Chandra, was the founder of the city which was named Lakshmanpura or Lakshmanawati after him. The Lakshman Tila is supposed to be a remnant of that period. At this site, during the course of an excavation of a sewer, antiquities and pottery of about the 6th century B.C. were discovered.

It is also said that in the environs of Lakshman Tila some Brahmin and Kshatriya families had settled. Later, with the coming of Muslims to India, families professing the new faith also settled here. In the early mediaeval period the Sheikhs and the Pathans claimed Zamindari over areas lying between the Residency and the Gol Darwaza. The tomb of Sheikh Meena, a Muslim saint, born in 1470 A.D. also belongs to this period. It is said that the Sheikhs built a fort at the site which was later known as the Machchhi Bhavan. Its architect was a Hindu named Lakhna, and the building was named Kila Lakhna after him. And from this was derived the name Lakhnau, i.e. modern Lucknow.

In the 6th century, when the Mughals conquered India, Lucknow also fell into their hands. Akbar took a great liking to the place, and since then it has been growing steadily. Abul Fazal, in *Ain-i-Akbari*, pays glowing tributes to the pleasant surroundings, excellent climate and rich produce of Lucknow. At this time was also built the Akbari Darwaza, the southern gate of Chowk. Jehangir, Akbar's son, is said to have built the Nadan Mahal, a beautiful mosque.

In the 18th century, Saadat Ali Khan founded the Oudh Dynasty of the Nawabs and made his entry into Lucknow, which was at that time dominated by the Sheikhs.

The maker of Lucknow was the fourth Nawab, Asaf-ud-daula, who transferred the capital of Oudh from Faizabad to Lucknow in 1775. In his time, the Lucknow court reached its highest splendor and no court in India could rival its extravagance and pomp. To this magnificent court crowded poets, philosophers, musicians, and adventures of all kinds. It was during his reign that fine living and culture found their finest expression, and the court became the center, the focal-point of poetry and music, and of courtly Urdu. His successors carried on the traditions of Asaf-ud-daula and succeeded in leaving a rich cultural heritage to after times.

The last Nawab Wajid Ali Shah was taken prisoner in 1857 and Oudh passed into the hand of British East India Company. The monuments of Lucknow bear ample witness to the struggle of Lucknow in 1857, which was both tragic and heroic.

The long reign of the Nawabs has left its deep impact' on the language, manners and the arts of this second largest city of the State. To this day Lucknow is considered a center of Muslim culture, Urdu language, Kathak dance and Thumri singing.

Nawabs Asaf-ud-daulah and Wajid Ali Shah had a taste for fine arts which flowered specially during the reign of the latter. Urdu language, Urdu drama and Ghazal acquired a refinement, which remains a typical feature of Lucknow culture to this day. In music, Lucknow excelled in the Thumri style of singing and, in dance, the Lucknow Gharana (school) of Kathak acquired a finesse which was never excelled. Wajid Ali Shah, himself an accomplished dancer and musician patronized these arts.

A very popular form of entertainment at the court were the shows of the Bhands, a group of professional jesters, who would regale the audience with dance and music, alternating with comic interludes which were a medley of mimicry, improvised, wit, and comic observations on life and manners. Their wit, sometimes bawdy, had a point to it; they were licensed clowns and caricaturists who enjoyed the same freedom in mocking the vanities and pretensions of the rich as the fool did in the Elizabethan England and the cartoonist does in the world of today.

Lucknow has been well-known as the home of Urdu language and poetry. Lucknow's special contribution to Urdu poetry lies in the domain of Marsiya, a kind of epic-elegiac poem dealing with the martyrdom of Imam Husain and members of his family. Anis and Dabir were the two best exponents of this kind of poetry. Lucknow has made no mean achievement in the sphere of Ghazal the commonest form of Urdu poetry. Lucknow and Delhi have for ever been rival centers of Urdu poetry, extremely jealous of each other's pre-eminence in this field. This style of poetry was essentially courtly and set more store by external embellishment, grace and verbal depth of feeling. Hence it suffers in some measure in comparison with the best that Delhi has contributed to Urdu poetry. Lucknow's most outstanding achievement consists, however, in the evolution of a brand of spoken Urdu; polished, urbane and of extreme delicacy and grace. A fact that is often overlooked is that this language was as much the possession of the Hindus as of the Muslims.

A favorite pastime of those days, which has survived to our own time, was the Mushairas, a gathering of poets who met to recite their verses before large and appreciative audiences which repeated each verse as it came from the lips of the poet. These frequent meets did much to foster in the people a love for, and an intelligent interest in, poetry. Poetry no longer remained the exclusive concern of the court and the nobility; it 'came home to the business and bosoms' of the generality of men.

In the time of Wajid Ali Shah, Kathak, the most important dance form of Northern India, won patronage. It was during his time that the Lucknow Gharana of Kathak acquired a stylist form. The founders of the school were Thakur Prasad and his father, Prakshji; master of rasdhari tradition of Kathak.

Wajid Ali Shah was so taken up with the skill of Thakur Prasad that he became his pupil. This family of dancers produced many brilliant exponents of the art. Two of Thakur Prasad's sons, Bindadin and Kalka Prasad, acquired great fame. Bindadin was gifted with poetic talent. He composed numerous thumris, and bhajans which became an integral part of Kathak Nritya, Kalka Prasad, on the other hand, excelled in rhythm. The two brothers made Kathak precise and at the same time saturated with rasa.

In the 19th century, the Nawabs set up a theater for the performance of opera ballets in the court of Lucknow. From this can be traced the origin of Urdu drama and stage. In the court of Wajid Ali Shah several dance dramas were performed-all set to music. These opera cum-ballet performances were a mixture of Kathak technique of dance, the Rasalila form of classical music, adapted to higher forms and stage technique. Wajid Ali Shah's first enterprise was Radha Kanhaiya Nataka.

A remarkable feature of life in those times was the cultural fusion of the two major communities, the Hindus and the Muslims. Nowhere else in India did the two communities mingle together so well; nowhere else they have lived in such a spirit of harmony and give-and-take. That is why the culture that developed here was a fine blend of the cultures of these two communities. A love of fine living, hospitality, urbanity, courtesy and good manners are some of the marks of this culture, which give to a man from Lucknow his distinctive stamp.

As one saunters about through the streets and by lanes of Lucknow, memory takes one gently by the hand and "Makes him peep through the blanket of the past". Every nook and corner of Lucknow, every park, palace or mausoleum, the scattered ruins choir where the sweet birds sang is all reminiscent of Nawabi time; they bring up visions of that dreaming world of yesterday and the day before. If the great Imambara stands today as an undying monument to the munificence of Nawab Asaf-ud-daulah as also to his great love of architecture, the rows of yellow buildings in Kaiserbagh bring crowding upon one's mind pictures of the loves and intrigues, the romance and the pageantry of the royal 'harem' of Wajid Ali Shah.

Lucknow in recent years has become a cosmopolitan town, with a remarkable diversity of cultures, races, communities, in its population. But the influx of people from outside and the impact of modern influences have not succeeded in destroying the distinctive character of Lucknow. Lucknow has in itself all the attractions of a period picture, its buildings, its manners and traditions all being of that period; its character was always Nawabi and it still remains so to a large extent. The old and the new here jostle; old traditions have not been swamped by modern currents; rather they have assimilated the newer influences. This has resulted in a synthesis of the old and the new. Lucknow is just the right size to enable its people to escape the small-town mentality and yet to retain that personal touch which is to be found in big cities. The Lucknow culture has an unmistakable flavour of its own; it combines emotional warmth and the intimacy of personal relationships with a high degree of sophistication. Lucknow still retains an old-world spaciousness; it has an air of leisureliness, of care-free gaiety; its population represents rather a pageant of holiday-makers than a crowd of workers and toilers, trying desperately to earn a living.

Hazratganj : Ganjing-strolling along the fashionable Hazratganj in the evening is a popular pastime. Here readymade clothing, mill cloth, books, household appliances and implements furniture and handicrafts, restaurants, coffee houses, and cinemas. The General Post Office (GPO) is at one end along with Christ Church Intermediate College.

Hotel Clarks Avadh

Council House

Residency

Chota Imambara

15

Of Shopping Interest

Nazirabad : Cane baskets, shoemakers, cut-piece shops, crockery and cooking utensils, button shop, chikan and zari work, type-writer rental shop.

Aminabad : The largest and best known shopping center in Lucknow. Here one can buy "from a pin to an elephant."

Latouche Road : (Re-named Gautam Buddha Marg but generally known by the earlier name given for the Governor who built the road). Center for guns and ammunition, tinsmiths, cycle shops, steel cabinets and wardrobes, paint, rough carpentry, charpais, hardware stores and electrical shops.

Kaiserbagh Circus : Opticians, shoe-makers, vegetables, fruits, meat and fish market and hotels where food can be made to order for large parties.

Aminabad Park: (Address of shops facing the open square of Aminabad). Shops include the U.P. Jails Depot, selling handicrafts and cotton carpets made by prisoners, chemists, cloth shops, knitting wool, stationery and chappal (sandals) sellers.

Refugee Market: Part of Aminabad Park has been taken up by three lines of shops known as the Refugee Market with stalls selling cloth, cut-pieces, buttons, knitting wool, embroidered kamizes (Punjabi style shirts), chappals, sun-glasses, bangles and other miscellaneous articles. Across the main street from the Refugee Market will be found the perfumers, luggage shops and goldsmiths. Nearby Gwynne Road are tin trunks and locks.

Amin-ud-daula Park: Here one may find linoleum and woven mats, a large Bata shop for shoes, more cloth shops, particularly Griha Bhandar and Cali Cloth and a cloth-printing firm. At the far end of this park is one of the most ornate of Lucknow's old mansions. The Park is popularly known as Jhandawalla Park because of the flagpole in the centre.

Shri Ram Road: Tiny but important for fancy toweling and drapery fabrics from Bombay Dyeing, a good socks and shorts shop. Mehra's a well stocked paint store, rope, kerosene, tobacco, hookahs, dry fruit and vanaspati (vegetable shortening) will all be found on Shri Ram Road.

Garbar Jhala : A collection of tiny stalls where nearly everything small can be found- bangles, nose-rings plastic caning, mothballs, rolling-pins, cheap plastic toys, balloons all far cheaper than they are at Hazrat Ganj if one has the ability to bargain.

Chowk Bazar: The oldest bazaar of the city is Chowk. The most interesting street is known as 'Gol Darwaza' (round door) Khunkhunji, one of the largest goldsmiths, is just before the arch. Down the street are chikan workshops, woodblock carvers, gold thread embroidery, masks and theatrical costumes, a perfume factory and, at the far end, a store dealing in clay toys. On certain days of the week, in many small shops men will be found pounding silver into then sheets to decorate sweets.

Super Market or Naya Bazar : Across the Lal Bagh Methodist Church and in Lal Bagh park, Naya Bazar has been built. Under one roof government contractors have gathered a variety of goods. Foods, toys, textiles, utensil' s and general merchandise are available here.

Daliganj : On the Daliganj side of the Iran Bridge will be found charpais (rope beds), bamboos of all lengths and girths and bamboo ladders.

Nakhas : On Sunday morning, one section of Victoria Road is open to sellers of live geese, ducks and other birds and animals, old crockery, brass and copper and all sorts of surprises.

16

Lalit Kala Akademi and its Aims

The Lalit Kala Akademi of Uttar Pradesh, being proud of its artistic and cultural heritage, has extended its patronage in fostering and co-ordinating activities in the sphere of the visual as well as plastic arts.

The Akademi aims at promoting artists and encouraging their creative talents by arranging exhibitions of their work, setting up a permanent gallery of paintings and sculptures, as well as publishing literature on art. By these endeavours it hopes to increase people's interest in art and to revive folk art, besides promoting research in art.

The Akademi has held several exhibitions since it began functioning, besides two showings of foreign artists. They have shown tempers paintings, water colours, oils and murals.

The Akademi also shares the worldwide interest in the trends in modern art. In view of this fact they exhibited 43 contemporary paintings from Yugoslavia, which represented a tradition of rich expressiveness, and a near sensual love of form and colour.

These paintings showed that much of modern art depicts fundamental social transformation, not being a mere portrayal of the subject observed.

The predominance of works having a kinship with the Modern School is very noticeable in the painting and sculpture sections. This may be due to the fact that there is apathy towards most traditional art, by the artist as well as the art-conscious.

The Akademi has held interesting and educative talks on the influence of the classical Rag and Raginis in Indian painting, and the origin and evolution of the Pahari School of Painting. They have discussed Moghul painting, Pal art, the art of Ajanta, the art of India, South-East Asia and the early phases in Indian Art. Much interest was shown in the vision form in Indian sculpture and Mural painting. It is an interesting and commendable effort that is being made by the Akademi which takes a genuine pleasure in putting forward the best and most versatile talent in the state.

The State Museum

It is an exciting experience to enter the portals of the State Museum at Lucknow, and to be confronted with the mummy of an Egyptian, with the papyrus bandages which the priests had enwrapped around it, still bright with hieroglyphic drawing.

Up the stairs to the first floor, you are confronted with fishes in the aquarium, bright flashes of vivid colours in the transparent void. Owls with hypnotic eyes perched up a dilapidated house, looking askance upon the visitor, so real that they seem to be aware of your intrusion.

Coloured birds on a tree are a splash of rainbow hues, snakes within and out of holes. A crocodile suddenly catches your eyes with its mouth a gap on a sandy bank, the saurian seems about to charge. A pride of tigers is seen in the forest; a she-wolf suckling her young in a barren, stony layer. You next see glittering coins displayed against black velvet, mute but eloquent reminders of the commerce and life of ages, not only of Oudh but also of many parts of India; bright metal images in the fore; exquisite gems of miniature painting as in quiet and sober surroundings.

Figures and motifs carved in wood; tall door frames medieval Hindu buildings, with the delicate tracery of the wood-worker's chisel are some of the sights which await you at the new Museum, which was declared open by the Late Prime Minister Pt. Nehru, on May 13th, 1964 in the pillared and imposing building at Banarasibagh.

The Museum set in the sylvan surrounding of the Zoological Gardens, took almost six years to construct and another year of hard and devoted work to shift and re-arrange exhibits collected over a period of hundred years.

17

The Perfume World

Everyone knows the story of how Empress Nur Jahan noticed a little oil floating in her bath, which led to the discovery of Otto of rose.

It is said that, taking the clue from his queen's bath, the Emperor Jehangir ordered the manufacture of perfume from rose petals, and some of the courtiers were encouraged to the making of otto. But the making of this perfume on an industrial basis began at Bharwana in Aligarh, where the soil and the climate are conducive to the growtn of roses. Ghazipur also became known for rose growing and the making of *attar* and rose-water from flowers.

Perfumers India and Asgar Ali are Famous for Perfumes and Itar

It is believed that the Arabs were the first to obtain perfume by means of distillation. The still of alembic is well-known all over the world, but it is less generously recognised that alembic is an Arabic word meaning still, which is established by research to have been in use in the 15th-17th centuries. It was in this period that Arabia became famed for its perfumes in Europe, and there are many allusions too in the literature of the times, including Shakespeare.

It would be a gigantic task to describe the whole range of *attars*, and flowers, so a few famous ones are mentioned.

Khus (Vertivert) - It is distilled from the root of a kind of a grass found in various parts of U.P. and also in other parts of India, and the mobile industry has to go to those places during the winter months.

Keora (Padanus Odoratissimus) - It is abundantly available in Orissa and so the portable distillery is sent there every year. The price remains fluctuating from year to year. A thousand flowers are put into the alembic at one time, the resulting water is known as '*hazara*', and if two thousand are used it is '*do hazara*', and so on. But distillers hardly use more than two thousand at a time.

Chameli - A kind of Jasmine has made Jaunpur famous. Apart from Attar Chameli, a speciality of Jaunpur is Chameli oil. This is obtained by placing layers of Til seed (Sesme L. Sea mum indicum) and chameli flowers alternatively, changing the spent flowers every day, until it is considered that the seeds have been saturated with the right amount of fragrance. The seeds are then put through a bullock-driven oil mol (ghani or kohlu) and the oil is extracted. The oil thus extracted is said to retain all the essential qualities, which may be lost if mechanical expellers are used. Chameli oil is widely used for various medicinal purposes and also as popular hair oil. Jaunpur has kept its legendary fame. But Lucknow has superseded the former in the making

The Medical College

not only of Attar Chameli and chameli oil, but all the other attars and oils.

Perfumes have been in use in India as in other countries from a long time. We find mention of sandal, camphor; saffron and so many other aromatic ingredients in many of our ancient books. They must have used them as pastes, since now-a-days they use turmeric paste and red or white sandal wood paste.

Quite early in the very beginning of the 19th century the Late Asghar Ali, founder of the firm of Messers. Asghar Ali Mohommad Ali, Lucknow, started his experiments in making *attar* that would have the qualities of long-lasting fragrance and of scenting the air. Thus, he used sandal oil musk, ambergris agar, saffron and other aromatic spices and herbs both indigenous and imported and was first able to make 'hina', attar of low Sonia flowers with the addition of several ingredients mentioned above, evolving a process of his own. Hina was previously made as just another purely floral extract based on sandal oil.

Lucknow is, on the whole, essentially an abode of people, refined and relaxed. The city is full of local colour and atmosphere, and devoid of the drabness and anxiety of industrialisation. It is the home town of leading Hindi writers and its serenity and spaciousness have attracted scientists of international standing. Except intellectual pursuits, it seems the pattern of life in the city cannot be otherwise.

18

Handicrafts

Clay models and toys of Lucknow are becoming popular in foreign countries. Orders for artistic clay models have been received here from the U.K., the U.S.A. and the Western countries. Local artists excel in making clay models of fruits and vegetables, bazaar scenes, marriage processions and certain aspects of village life.

Chikan : The Hall Mark of Lucknow's Craftsmanship

Chikan work, the pride of Lucknow's needle-workers and the favourite exclusive sartorial vogue of royalty and nobility in the olden days, has, after long years of vicissitudes, been restored to stability and progress.

In the haleyon days, master craftsmen permanently attached to royal palaces and aristocratic homes used to vie with one another in producing finer specimens of *dupalli topi, angarakha* and *kurta* and earned due rewards in gifts and reputation.

When, with the advent of the British, fortune turned its face away from the Nawabs of Oudh, evil days befell their favourite dress-makers too, with the loss of patronage.

For decades, the chikan worker had to adopt his craft to the tastes of the middle classes and to be content with the poorer returns he could now expect. The quality of the art deteriorated and the demand dwindled, and the helpless band of artists looked on helplessly as the more intricate stitches and finer designs dwindled into oblivion.

After the attainment of Independence, the Government in 1947 formulated a scheme to resuscitate and rehabilitate the ebbing industry, known by the pompous name of Rajakiya Chikan Karhai Yojana. The scheme had four objectives; regular employment of workers on fair wages; improvement in the standard of workmanship: revival of the traditional motifs and introduction of new patterns and development of marketing facilities in and outside the country.

It started modestly with a grant of Rs. 50,000 for commercial operation. The first few years were utilised in making contact with workers, enrolling them and evolving designs.

The scheme deals with cottage workers directly. Workers are mostly 'Burqa Clad' women, guided by women supervisors. The artisans are given work on prescribed wages. There is arrangement for distribution, collection and payment of wages at the worker's homes.

There is no middleman, and the worker gets expert quality technical guidance in making standard quality goods. The workers are encouraged to improve their workmanship and higher wages are paid for finer pieces.

There are special arrangements for booking orders for individual customers and care is taken to execute these to the satisfaction of customers.

Arrangements have also been made to extend the scheme to rural areas. Workers have been enrolled at Kakori, Bijnor and Rhushalganj. It is now planned to cover the place within a radius of 15 miles from the city where there are sufficient number of workers.

A Common Facility Center (Chikan) was established in1961-62, where technical advice regarding cutting, sewing, designing, embroidery, washing, finishing and marketing is given free to co-operative societies and private individuals. During the first year of the Third Plan, 125 artisans were helped, while during the second year 504.

Efforts are being made to form co-operative societies. Financial assistance and grants-in-aid were given to four of such societies in 1961-62 and they have started production. Six more societies were registered in 1962-63, financial assistance has also been sanctioned.

A Central Handicrafts Co-operative Society has also been formed to undertake purchase of raw material for the primary societies and sale of their finished goods. A sales-cum-showroom has been started under the

Specimen of Brass Industry

Central Handicrafts Society at Chhota Imambara, which is gaining popularity.

The scheme has revived the industry and its reputation as a fine craft has been re-established.

19

Chinhat Crockery

The Pilot Pottery Project-popularly known as the 'Chinhat Crockery Factory'- was set up in January 1959, at Chinhat, a small and speedily-developing village about seven miles from Lucknow. It was started with a total investment of three lakhs of rupees by the Planning Research and Action Institute (P.R.A.I.) under its experimental programme to ascertain whether small-scale industries employing modern techniques could be non-officially run in rural areas, so as to be eventually owned by rural artisans and people.

The factory is situated at a place where the cluster of huts in the hamlet is relatively thin, affording a full view of the adjoining landscape to the visitor. In all, about 150 workers, including those on a contract basis, are employed in its various sections apart from about fifteen members on the staff of offices. Some forty to fifty buyers visit the factory every working day, between 8 a.m. and 5 p.m.

A colourful jumble of pieces of crockery, designed and decorated in variegated hues, greet the eyes of the visitor on entering the store-room. Showcases, along the verandah, are arranged with the first-rate goods for the factory products have been classified into four grades according to their quality, symmetry and finish.

Outstanding amongst the pieces turned out by the stone-ware unit and the earthenware unit are tea-sets, coffee sets, lemon-sets, flower-vases, 'kundis' and jars, decoration exhibits and lamp-bases and the bowls of an appreciable variety of shape and size.

The Pilot Pottery Project at Chinhat serves the purposes of field laboratory when trials for developing different varieties of articles are carried out. Accordingly, the Planning Research and Action Institute consider the possibility of developing table wares and crockery articles with decorations and designs having an indigenous touch. Such articles can be manufactured in small workshops and provide opportunities for the employment for talented rural youth and also add to the productive capacity of the rural areas.

Side by side with the designing of articles, it is very necessary that glaze on articles should be such that they are acceptable. Experiments are being conducted to find out what material should be used for glazing the articles keeping in view the requirements of a rural industry.

The low cost of the raw material and variety of individual articles in pottery industry make it ideal one for being organised on decentralised basis. The P.R.A.I. is currently engaged in experimentation in this direction also.

It may be mentioned that apart from producing beautifully designed pottery ware for sophisticated buyers and providing employment to nearly 100 persons, the project has contributed significantly to the popularisation and production of stone wares in the Government's unit as well as amongst enterprising potters.

20

Lucknow's Beauty: A Foreign-Eye View

To the newcomer the city of Wajid Ali Shah on the Gomati presents many unique features, and a boy-like attitude to please, to be seen and heard. There are many things a boy could be criticized for; dirty nails for instance, unruly hair or some other. If you want to criticise Lucknow, it is easy. Lucknow luckily is on the list of foreign visitors. True, the city is lacking in unique temples and the gorgeous splendors of the Mughals. Lucknow is peculiarly plebeian, despite its aristocratic tradition of exaggerated fineness in manners and modes of speech. If you are out just to have a good time that is easy too. Recently I had the pleasure of interviewing three young girls from the Soviet Union, in these days of quick travel, Lucknow daily experiences the thrill of welcoming visitors from every corner of the globe. The three Russian girls were, however, unique themselves, although coming from a vast and powerful state; they were simple as the proverbial Scythian. It was easy for the small boy to impress them. Blue-eyed Anita Beira is a teacher. Tussled haired Galine Arkipore is an interpreter, and a Komemol, i.e., Larissa Gallant a

Martyrs' Memorial

young Engineer serious looking as her business. This is their first visit to India and happily they flew in from Delhi. The drive from the airport to Hazratganj is pleasant, and one by one they enjoyed the sights without unnecessary guides or instructors. They rambled among the vast Imambara, Mosques and Tombs, and the numerous parks and gardens; what they saw was India, in a state of transition.

At the recently-created Martyrs' Memorial, which is, square pillar crowned with a lotus bud, they contemplated the sacrifices, trials and tribulations which the young had gone through, and which is recent history. The upraised trunk of the sky-gazing elephants is symbolic of the nation's aims and ambitions. The sculptures in the National Botanical Gardens attracted them greatly and also the garden itself. There is an aura of mystery and antiquity in the gardens of Lucknow, something far away and remote. It is precisely because of this that they are liked by visitors who are familiar with conventional gardens.

21

Colvin Taluqdars' College

Colvin Taluqdar's College one of the oldest and premier institutions of Lucknow has Classes I to XII for boys. It is Bilingual providing parallel English and Hindi classes. The college conducts two public examinations at the end of classes X and XII, the High School and the Intermediate examination, respectively, of the U.P. Board of High School and Intermediate Education Allahabad. Admissions take place on the basis of a written test and an interview in July every year. The minimum age for admission to class one is five years and the college sets a maximum age for each class.

The college has a beautiful campus in an area of about 80 acres on the banks of the river Gomati and just opposite Lucknow University. Its extensive playing fields, impressive college building, spacious boarding houses, swimming pool and squash court, along with the rich traditions of the college, gives it a distinctive status.

Sir Auckland Colvin, one time Lt. Governor of Oudh, conceived the idea of the school as a place for educating wards of the court and sons of Taluqdars (land-owners). With the help of the Taluqdars of Oudh,

Colvin Taluqdars' College

who provided the capital, the foundation was laid in 1892. Admission to the school was limited to the sons or near relations of Taluqdars and for the first forty years the school was running exclusively for and on behalf of the Taluqdar community.

In 1933, the school was reorganised into an Intermediate Arts College. The fees were lowered and admission thrown open to all. In 1945, Intermediate Science classes were started with the help of the parent body, the British Indian Association.

Today the college is meeting the challenge of the time and is a full member of the India Public School Conference. Compulsory games, common messing. effective house and prefect systems, co-curricular activities and equal emphasis on academic results have laid the foundation of an all-round education to produce young men proud of their national heritage and culture, able to shoulder responsibility and to fill positions in all walks of national life.

22

University of Lucknow : Its Affiliated Colleges

On the northern bank of River Gomati stand the Indo-Saracenic-styled buildings of the University of Lucknow, once popularly known by the name Canning College.

The University, which is both residential and affiliating, houses five faculties-Arts, Commerce, Law, Medicine and Science, besides the following degree colleges affiliated to it:-

1. Bappa Sri Narain Vocational Degree College.
2. Mahatma Gandhi Girls School.
3. D.A.V. College.
4. I.T. College.
5. Jai Narain College.
6. Jubilee Girl's College.

7. Karamat Hussain Muslim Girls' College.
8. Millennium College.
9. Kanya Kubj Vocational College.
10. Kanya Kubj College.
11. Khunkhunji Girl's Degree College.
12. Loreto Convent Degree College.
13. Lucknow Christian College.
14. Mahila Vidyalaya.
15. Nari Shiksha Niketan.
16. National College.
17. Navyug Kanya Vidyalaya.
18. Shri Jai Narain College.
19. Shia College.
20. Modern Police School.
21. Shashi Bhushan Balika Vidyalaya.
22. Modern School, Aliganj.

The history of the University begins as early as 1866 when a Taluqdar supported High School of the city was declared a college and affiliated to the Calcutta University for the degree of B.A. and later on for Law. Gradually this college got the recognition of the State and in 1905 the Government of U.P. purchased the Nawabi garden then known as Badshahbagh, for, construction of University building to be designed by Sir Swinton Jacob. In 1920, the Isabella Thoburn College and the K.G's Medical College and the Canning College were joined to form the University.

Children's Museum and Library

Motilal Nehru Memorial Society's Children Museum is situated on the Station Road, adjacent to Ravindralaya. The Museum, which provides diverse attractions to the children has a well-equipped playground and organizes from time to time exhibition programmes of music and drama and classes of music etc. for them.

It has also the distinction of having a well-equipped library of over 8000 books specially written, designed and bound for children in the country and abroad.

Nasiria Library

Near the Rakabganj railway crossing is the Nasiria Library. It has about 11,000 volumes most of which are rare manuscripts. They are the remains of the private collection of Mufti Saiyid Muhammad Quli which had changed to survive the Mutiny of 1857. The library gets an annual grant from the Government.

Railway Research Design and Standards Organisation

Railway Research Designs and Standards Organisation was opened by the Ministry of Railway at Lucknow in 1957 for specialising in various branches of Railway engineering. The organisation has established its colony at Alambagh in an area of about 400 acres and has nearly a staff of 2,100 persons including officers.

The main function of this institution is research and designing. Research work deals with mechanical, electrical, signaling, chemical, and engineering transportation.

Design work includes designing of permanent ways, rail sleepers, rail fastening, points and crossing and all other fittings required to make a track. It also designs bridge girders and large structures. There is even an architectural section to design important buildings.

The organisation also deals with many other problems, efficiency of railway and its competition with air and road traffic.

Central Drug Research Institute

The Central Drug Research Institute in Lucknow is housed in the old Chhatar Manzil buildings opposite Begum Hazrat Mahal Park. This beautiful building which carries many legends behind its name and many stories of mentioning that its ground-floor is said to be submerged deep into the water was built by Claude Martin in 1784.

This institute sponsored by the Council of Scientific Research has multifarious functions. Besides the promotion of drug research, in general which includes testing and standardising drugs discovered in the institute, it provides expert advice to various agencies regarding production of these drugs and disseminates other scientific knowledge relating there. It also provides facilities and advice to such Industries, Universities and Scientists etc, which are either not in a position to carry out certain investigations relating to drugs or complete the same.

The important sections of the institute are Biochemistry, Chemistry, Microbiology, Parasitology, Clinical and Botany etc. It has also an animal house for its experimental work, a little away from its main buildings.

23

Nursery Schools, Intermediate Colleges

The Nagar Mahapalika, Lucknow provides free primary education in every area within the municipal limits. It also maintains a couple of Junior High Schools along with two Inter-colleges, i.e., Kashmiri Mohalla Girl's Intermediate College and the Aminabad Intermediate College for boys.

Some of the other Nursery Schools and Intermediate Colleges being run by the Christian missionaries and other private institutions are as below:-

NURSERY SCHOOLS

1. Bal Vidya Mandir, Opp. Charbagh Railway Station, Lucknow.
2. Cathedral School, Hazratganj, Lucknow.
3. Christ Church Nursery School, Hazratganj, Lucknow.

4. City Montessori Schools of Jagdish Gandhi, Branches : Station Road, Rajendra Nagar, Maha Nagar, Hazratganj and Raja Bazar, etc.

5. Lal Bagh Nursery School, Lal Bagh, Lucknow.

6. Leelawati Bal Griha, Moti Nagar, Lucknow.

7. Loreto Convent Nursery School, Mahatma Gandhi Marg, Lucknow.

8. Lucknow Montessori School, Mahatma Gandhi Marg, Lucknow.

9. Municipal Nursery School, Lucknow.

10. Playway School, City Station Road, Lucknow.

11. St. Mark's School, Sadar, Lucknow.

12. St Peter's Day School, Station Road, Lucknow.

13. St. Bernadette School, Chowk, Lucknow.

14. Tiny Tots, Lucknow.

15. Mahatma Gandhi School.

INTERMEDIATE COLLEGES

Christ Church Inter College: Founded and being run by the Anglican Church, this institution holds classes from I to XII for both boys and girls. The medium of instruction is English.

Colvin Taluqdar's College: Founded by Sir Auckland Colvin, one time Lt. Governor of Oudh for educating wards of the court and sons of Taluqdars, the institution started to function formally in 1892. The admission was limited to the sons or near relations of

Taluqdars and the school was conducted for and on behalf of the Taluqdar community for the first forty years but after its reorganisation into an Intermediate Arts College in 1933, the admission was then open to all and fees were lowered. During 1945, with the help of the British India Association, Intermediate Science classes were started.

The college with its extensive 80 acres compound on the bank of Gomati, opposite Lucknow University has today extensive playing fields, beautiful swimming pool, squash and tennis-courts and big and imposing buldings. The institution is holding classes from I to XII and is bi-lingual providing parallel classes both in English and Hindi. Age for admission into class I is five years. The college has also prescribed a maximum age for each class.

Dayanand Anglo Vedic College: An institution for boys which holds classes from III to XII in Hindi medium for boys. It is affiliated with the University of Lucknow for the BA Degree. The college has hostel facilities also.

Karamat Hussain Girl's College: Situated on the Faizabad Road it holds classes from I to XII and runs in two shifts. It also holds classes for B.A. and Degree Section, which is affiliated with the University of Lucknow.

La Martiniere College for Boys: With classes III to XII for boys in English medium. It prepares students for the Indian School Certificate examination.

Founded in accordance with the will of Major General Claud Martin. The college is administered by a board of Governors. The La Martiniere boys participated in the defense of the Residency during the siege of 1857. The college had been given battle honours.

It also provides hostel accommodation for 250 boys.

Loreto Convent College: Founded by the Roman Catholic church, the college runs classes from Kindergarten to XII for girls in English medium.

It is affiliated with the University of Lucknow for the BA Degree.

St. Agnes Loreto High School: Classes K.G. to X for girls in English medium. Managed by the Loreto Convent.

St. Francis' College for Boys: Founded By Rev. Fr. Narbert, O.F.M. Cap. an Italian father and managed by the Catholic Diocese of Lucknow. It runs classes from K.G. to XI in English medium and prepares the students for Indian School Certificate examinations.

Mahila Vidyalaya : Classes II to XII in Hindi medium for Girls. It is affiliated with the University of Lucknow for the BA degree.

Mount Carmel Convent School : Classes K.G. to X, medium of instruction up to class V is English. From class VI to X it is bi-lingual providing parallel English and Hindi classes.

Maha Nagar Boy's High School: Classes III to X-Bi-lingual providing parallel classes both in English and Hindi.

Nari Shiksha Niketan: Classes I to XII Hindi medium for girls. It is affiliated with the University of Lucknow for the B.A. classes.

Shashi Bhushan Balika Vidyalaya : Classes II to XII-Hindi medium, for girls. It is affiliated with the University of Lucknow for the BA classes.

24

Social Service Agencies

There is a network of social service institutions in the city run by the voluntary organisations. Many of them have the patronage of the Government in the shape of financial assistance. A few of the more prominent ones are as below:

Nari Sewa Samiti: The main aim of the Nari Sewa Samiti is the upliftment of women and children both in the rural and urban areas through its activities which include every sphere of social service.

The Samiti is currently running the educational institutions viz, the Zenana Park Primary School in Aminabad, the Bal Shiksha Niketan and Nari Shiksha Niketan, the last two being located in the Women's institute at Kaiser Bagh. It has established a production center where women are trained in Home crafts and a showroom where the goods produced at the centre are put up for display and sale.

Young Women's Christian Association : Y.W.C.A. is a Christian association devoted to the cause of young women. Its activities are multifarious. The Association is running a Youth Hostel where young ladies can safely put up at a very moderate cost. A team of voluntary workers including a doctor holds every Wednesday a clinic at Sultanpur Road, eight miles from Lucknow. It also holds literacy classes and teaches useful handicrafts to women. Occasionally it also deputes its social workers and other voluntary workers to help the programme of other organisations.

U.P. Council of Child Welfare: The U.P. Council of Child Welfare is the State branch of the India Council for Child Welfare in New Delhi. The Prime Minister is the President of this institution and the Governor is the president of the State branch. The Council has the distinction of being the only institution which has established a creche for the children of working women in Lucknow, i.e., Leelawati Bal Grih at Moti Nagar, Aishbagh station. The Association has organised recreation centres in nine mohallas.

Some of the social institutions are :-

1. *Anjuman Islahul Muslem in Aminabad*: This institution has one orphanage and three schools including an Industrial School.
2. *King's Poor House, Tulsi Das Marg:* This institution provides free clothing and shelter to the destitutes.
3. *Municipal Sewa Sadan, Tahsin Ganj :* Its main aim is rehabilitation of beggars and destitutes of all types.
4. *Sri Ram Industrial Orphanage:* Orphan children are provided free food, clothing and shelter without any distinction of caste, creed, colour and sex. They are also provided vocational training.

5. *Deaf and Dumb School and Teacher's Training College, Aish Bagh*: School provides vocational training to the deaf and the dumb and also trains teachers for them.

6. *Indian Village Service*: The main aim of this institution is to improve rural living through intensive programme in small industries and agriculture and bridge the gulf between rural and urban life.

Medical Services

The following hospitals and clinics provide free treatment to the sick, most of them have special arrangement for the private patients :-

Hospitals Run by the Government

Allopathic :

1. Balrampur Hospital, Golaganj.
2. Civil Hospital, Soochna Bhawan Buildings.
3. Dufferin Hospital, Golaganj-A female hospital specially useful for maternity cases.
4. Victoriaganj Hospital.

Homoeopathic:

National Homoeopathic College.

Ayurvedic and Unani College:

State Ayurvedic Hospital, Turiaganj.

Hospital and Clinics Providing Specialist Treatment

1. Distt. T.B. Clinic, Rajendra Nagar.
2. Leprosy Hospital, Nisatganj.

3. Man Sarover Eye Clinic, Station Road.

4. Nur Manzil, Lal Bagh : It is a Psychiatric Center maintained by the Methodist Church.

   Programmes in small industries and agriculture and bridge the gulf between rural and urban life.

HOSPITAL

1. Mahatma Gandhi Memorial Hospital, Shahmina Road.

2. Queen Mary's Hospital, Shahmina Road-A female hospital-Branch of Mahatma Gandhi Memorial Hospital- A training centre for doctors and nurses.

3. Sanjay Gandhi Post Graduate Institute Rai Bareilly Road- Lucknow.

Hospitals and Clinics Run by Other Institutions

Fatima Maternity Clinic, Mahanagar: This clinic run by a Christian Missionary is a clinic for women and children.

MISCELLANEOUS

Military Hospital Cantonment:

Besides Military personnel it also admits civil patients under special circumstances or in cases of emergency.

Ambulance Service:

Ambulance services available in the following hospitals:-

1. Mahatma Gandhi Memorial Hospital

2. Queen Mary's Hospital

3. Balrampur Hospital

4. Civil Hospital or Shyam Prasad Mukerji Hospital
5. Nishat Hospital
6. Sahara Hospital.
7. Sanjay Gandhi Post Graduate Institute.

25

Vivekanand Polyclinic

The Vivekanand Poly Clinic has been established and run by the Rama Krishan Mission and is designed to be one of the most technically advanced hospitals in the country.

Though, the plans for the hospital are still under process and the work is in progress on all fronts, the hospital has started functioning with a modest strength of fifty six doctors and an army of social and paramedical workers, most of them specialists, trained and educated outside the country. So far, they have a hundred indoor beds.

The building of the hospital is a rare specimen of the modern architecture in which the Rajasthan marble has been liberally used to suit the need of the occasion and also project the grandeur and magnificence of the building.

This complex is designed to be air-conditioned and fully televised.

Vivekanand Polyclinic

26

Noor Manzil-Its Idea

Researches have now more than established that most of the human diseases originate in the mind. The advancement of Science, having added grace and glamour to human life, has at the same time made it more miserable and complex. These complexities are the root cause of all psychological riddles and mental tensions, which when translated into behaviour make the individual misfit in life and society.

The need and importance of psychiatric centres dawned in the West long ago with the result that almost every hospital and dispensary therein has a psychiatric wing besides numerous psychological bureaus and centres which provide specialist treatment in this sphere. But India even today is miles behind in this race.

As Dr. E. Stanley Jones traveled through India, he became convinced of the need of such a Centre in this country in view of the increasing psychological problems among people. It was many years ago that he conceived the idea of having this Centre.

During 1949 Dr. Jones had a chance to meet Dr. Dagmar Novell, a Swedish psychiatrist studying in the U.S.A. He invited her to share his venture. Dr. Novel officially opened Nur Manzil Psychiatric Center in December, 1950, for service to the mentally and emotionally sick. Since then, this Center has been under the able supervision and direction of many eminent doctors and psychologists as Dr. Even M. Hock of Basel, Switzerland, and James A. Stringham of, New York. During 1956, a building programme was undertaken for increasing the capacity of the institution. The next year Dr. Jones transferred the responsibilities for the Center to a Board of Governors under the Methodist Church in Southern Asia.

Nur Manzil Psychiatric Center offers treatment to patients and gives training doctors and nurses irrespective of race, religion and nationality. For treatment, versatile and most modern methods are used which include Individual Psychotherapy, Group Psychotherapy, Hypnosis, Counseling and Spiritual Therapy. Besides these, Electric Shock Therapy, Occupational Therapy and adjuncts to other forms of therapy.

This Center, the only one of its kind in India provides treatment both to indoor and outdoor patients. But the patients are seen by appointment only. This appointment can be made by mail, telephone, telegraph or in person. There is always a doctor on call in the Center. If he considers a case as an emergency, an appointment is made shortly. After the final consultation the doctor discusses the proposed treatment and gives an estimate as to the length of time that would probably be required. In general, in-patients require a minimum period of three months if not longer. The official in-patients capacity of the Center is 26 only.

Nur Manzil is a non-profit institution offering treatment to patients regardless of race, creed, religion and financial ability to pay. Both the poor patients and paying patients are treated alike and without any distinction within the limits of the Centers.

For the indoor patients there are arrangements of rooms. Every room has usually two beds and the patient has to pay - per bed per day. If a private room is desired by the patient he will have to pay per day. Air-conditioned rooms are also available. Room charges include food, room, bedding mattress, towels, utilities, ordinary medicines and routine nursing care. Extra charges have to be paid for lab tests, special medicines and X-ray. The atmosphere of this Psychiatric Center is quite serene and poised and the patient as well as his family and other attendants feel at home. Facilities are always encouraged to talk to doctors and other social workers regarding their relatives.

The employees of the Center are strictly forbidden to accept gratuities. People desiring to leave gratuities are directed to put them into the special box in the out-patient area or by giving the same to the Office Manager and receiving an official receipt. The money is distributed in July and Christmas.

Nur Manzil and has a reputation of its own not only in the country but also at the International level. Patients from other countries are also there for treatment.

27

Cinemas, Hotels and Other

1. Hind
   Bulaki Adda, Lucknow 2265578

2. Jagat 2614341
   Aminabad, Lucknow

3. Sahu Theatre, 2622235
   Sahu Bldg., Hazratganj, Lucknow

4. Shubham Theatre 2623570
   Cantt Road. Lalbagh, Lucknow

5. Sudershan 2450886
   Charbagh, Lucknow

6. Krishna 2455949
   Alambagh, Lucknow

7. Navelty Theatre 2616575
   Lal Bagh, Lucknow

8. Prakash 2260821
   N M Road, Lucknow

9.	Wave Cinemas Westend Mall, Gomti Nagar, Lucknow	4088788
10.	Novelty IInd Kapoorthala, Lucknow	2325369
11.	(Fun Republic) Zee Mall. Gomti Nagar, Lucknow	
12.	Sahara Ganj (PVR) Shahnajaf Road, Hazratganj, Lucknow	2505787
13.	(Inox) Riverside Mall, Gomti Nagar, Lucknow	

POLICE OFFICES

1.	Director General of Police	2208085
2.	Control Room	2221893,100
3.	IG Zone	2393300
4.	SSP and DIG Sapru Marg	2225984
5.	DIG Range	2225480
6.	SP City	2222217
7.	Police Head Quarters	2208596, 2201604 2208857
8.	SP (RA)	2228965
9.	SP (Trans Gomti)	2385969

KOTWALI

SP Traffic	2229669
Chowk	2223836
Hazratganj	2222555
CHOWKI	
Kaiserbagh	2222767
Aliganj	2324930

Alambagh	2451205
Banthra	2861661
Aminabad	2224635
Bakshi Ka Talab (05214)	298488
Bazar Khala	2269004
Gomti Nagar	2393400
Cantt	2480842
Gudamba	2361655
Chinhat	2315834
Kakori	2298230
Gazipur	2344900
MAL (919)	223222
Gosain Ganj	2836453
Nagram (918)	754
Hasan Ganj	2215352
Sarojini Nagar	2436600
Talkatora	2418718
Krishna Nagar	2470606
Thakurganj	2249991
Mahanagar	2385151
DGP Control	2208596
Mahila Thana	2211165
Vikas Nagar (Outpost)	2738398
Malihabad	2821223
Nakkhas (Outpost)	2260789
Mandiyaon	2362600
PGI (Outpost) (Extn. 100)	2440008
Mohanlal Ganj (05214)	221223
Bandariya Bagh (Outpost)	2226970
Naka	2222671
Aishbagh (Outpost)	2241222
Sahadat Ganj	2262556
Nishatganj (Outpost)	2389207
Wazir Ganj	2649556
Khurram Nagar (Outpost)	2328913
Police Lines	2781408

Alambagh	2451205
DCR	2782531
Itaunja (05212)	296227

STADIUM CLUB AND RESORTS

Ashiana Chancellor Club
Kanpur Road, Lucknow 2423347

Ansal Theatres and Club
Ashiana Colony, Lucknow 2423347

Baradari
Qaiserbagh, Lucknow 2622337

East End Mall
Gomti Nagar, Lucknow 40542700

Dream World
Lko. Knp. Highway, Lucknow 2327038

Charan's Club and Resorts
Opp. Akashwani, Fd. Rd. Lucknow 2815736

Genesius Club
9, Kursi Road, Lucknow 2361005

Lucknow Club
Ashok Marg, Lucknow 2275932

Lucknow Golf Club
Kalidas Marg, Lucknow 2239275, 2620631

Mohammad Bagh Club (MB Club)
M.G.Road, Lucknow 2480045

Scorpio Club
Off. Kursi Road, Gudamba, Lucknow 40691800

Nand Gaon Resorts
Faizabad Road, Lucknow 3293100

Oudh Gymkhana Club
Kaiserbagh, Lucknow 2615436

Press Club
Qaiserbagh, Lucknow
2620601

Rotary Club
Nazarbagh, Lucknow 2628178

Shivgarh Resorts
Thapar House, park Road, Lko 2238320

Surya Auditorium (Defence)
Cantt. Lucknow 2292955

Aamrapali Water Park
Shalimau Malihabad, Lucknow 2841033

Four Seasons Fun City
Rae Bareily Road, Lucknow 2618510

Babu K.D. Singh Stadium
MG Road, Lucknow 2623885

Sports College
Jankipuram, Lucknow 2377634

UTTAR PRADESH TOURIST OFFICES

UP State Tourism Development
Corporation Ltd
Paryatan Bhawan, C-13, Vipin Khand,
Gomti Nagar, Lucknow 2308916, 2308017

UP Tours
Hotel Gomti, 6, Sapru Marg, Lucknow
(For Reservation & Booking Schedule) 2612659

Regional Tourist Office
10, Station Road, Lucknow 2282112

State Information Bureau
Near Jawahar Bhawan, Ashok Marg,
Lucknow 2635544

Tourist Information Centre (U P Govt.)
Charbagh, Lucknow 2636173

Wild Life Information Centre
Wireless HQ, Mahanagar, Lucknow 2385761

GOVERNMENT GUEST HOUSES

State Guest House	2287318
UP State Guest House	2287488
VIP Guest House	2208620, 2208608
VVIP Guest House	2610076 , 2610051

AUDITORIUMS AND CULTURAL CENTRES

Bhat-Khande University
Rani Laxmi Bai Marg, Lucknow 2622928

Gandhi Bhawan Auditorium
M.G.Marg, Lucknow 2300598
Bhartendu Natya Academy
Gomti Nagar, Lucknow 2300598

Ganna Kisan Sansthan Auditorium
Dalibagh, Lucknow 2300598

Natya Kala Kendra
Kaiserbagh, Lucknow 2300598

Rai Umanath Bali Auditorium
Kaiserbagh, Lucknow 2614393

Ravindralaya
Charbagh, Lucknow 2355670

Surya Auditorium
Cantt., Lucknow 2292955

Udyan Vibhag Auditorium
Sapru Marg, Lucknow 2280277

U P Hindi Academy
Hazratganj, Lucknow 2614476

U P Sangeet Natya Academy
Gomti Nagar, Lucknow 2300023

Urdu Academy
Gomti Nagar, Lucknow 2395192

HOTELS

STD Code -0522

THE TAJ RESIDENCY HOTEL 393939
Vipin Khand, Gomti Nagar, Lucknow 2391201-3

HOTEL LA-PALACE PARK INN 4004040
6, Shahnajaf Road, Lucknow

HOTEL CLARKS AVADH 2620131-33
8, M.G. Marg, Lucknow 2616600-9

MOHAN HOTEL 2635717
Charbagh, Lucknow 2635797

HOTEL PICCADILY 4096000
Sector-B, Bara Birwa, Kanpur Road,
Lucknow

HOTEL DEEP AWADH 2684381-7
Nakahindola, Aminabad Road, Lucknow

HOTEL SAGAR INTERNATIONAL 2206601·5
14-A, Japling Road,
Opp. Buller Palace, Lucknow

HOTEL CHARAN INTERNATIONAL 2612516
16, Vidhan Sabha Marg, Lucknow 2612518

CAPOOR'S HOTEL 2623958
52, Hazratganj, Lucknow 2627262

GEMINI CONTINENTAL 4011111
10, Rani Laxmi Bai Marg. Lucknow 2200682

HOTEL COMFORT INN 2720984-88
TC-75V, Vibhuti Khand, Gomti Nagar;
Lucknow

LIFE STYLE HOTELS (P) LTD. 9415019728
BTC House, Daroga Khera,
Kanpur Road, Lucknow

HOTEL GOMTI (U.P. TOURISM) 2620624
6, Tej Bahadur Sapru Marg, Lucknow 2614284

DEEP HOTEL 2636441-18
5, Vidhan Sabha Marg, Lucknow

HOTEL SYONA RESIDENCY 2464644
Opp. Railway Station, 82, Charbagh,
Kanpur Road, Lucknow
(Detail on Col. Page No. 6)

HOTEL GLAXY INTERNATIONAL 6450861
Naka Hindola Crossing, Charbagh,
Lucknow

HOTEL SARANG 3919661
126.21, B.N.Road, Opp. Islamia College,
Lalbagh, Lucknow

HOTEL EUROPE PALACE 2636888
R-8, Behind Sharma Hotel, Charbagh,
Lucknow

HOTEL NAZNIN PALACE 2621175
38 Cantt. Road, Opp. Harmain Hospital,
Lucknow

EXECUTIVE GUEST HOUSE 2209804
13, M.M. Marg, Lucknow

DAYAL PARADISE 4059999
Vipul Khand-V, Gomti Nagar, Lucknow

HOTEL AMIT 238785
Nr. Indira Bridge, Nishatganj, Lucknow

HOTEL ANANT 3012209
16 Vidhansabha Marg, Lucknow 2624286

HOTEL DIMOND PALACE 2700777
Near Hotel Awadh International
Ismailganj, Faizabad Road, Lucknow

LODGES AND HOTELS IN LUCKNOW
(Reasonable Charges)
STD CODE - 0522

HOTEL MERA MANN 2638181-4
1, Station Road, Lucknow 2636175
(Detail Col. Page 10)

HOTEL VISHWANTH Charbagh, Lucknow	2450879 2452944
HOTEL AMAR PREET Charbagh, Lucknow	2456626 2455372
HOTEL TEKAREES INN 17/3, Ashok Marg, Lucknow	2202326 4016248
HOTEL TULSI Pandariba, Charbagh, Lucknow	2451626 2455425
HOTEL MAYUR Charbagh, Lucknow	2451 4048129
HOTEL MEZBAN INTERNATIONAL 92, G.B. Marg, Lucknow	2202953 2202954
PAL HOTEL Narhi Bazar, Lucknow (Detail page 107)	3200900
THE GRAND HOTEL 4, Lalbagh, Lucknow	2624229 2619661
MAYUR TOURIST LODGE 19, Mall Avenue, Lucknow	2239314 2236235
HOTEL SAMRAT Charbagh, Lucknow	2637705 2637732
HOTEL SHIMLA INN 140, G.B. Marg, Lucknow	2200106 2619824
HOTEL MANISHA 198/48, Ganesh Ganj, Lucknow	2682842 2681847

HOTEL GEETANJALI 2637378
Pandariba, Charbagh, Lucknow 2637311
YATRI HOTEL 2637681
7, Vijai Nagar, Lucknow 2681507

HOTEL DILEEP 2450996
42, Vidhan Sabha Marg, Lucknow

CENTRAL HOTEL 4015514
Opp. Jhande Wala Park, 4042424

Aminabad, Lucknow
BENGALI HOTEL 4008058

Charbagh, Lucknow 4015514
ROYAL INN 4048110-11
9. Shahnajaf Road, Lucknow 4007903
(Detail on Cover Front Inside)

HOTEL AMBER 2683201-3
Naka Hindola, Lucknow

RESTAURANTS

STD CODE - 0522

MARKS MEN RESTAURANT 2614252
2, Maqbara Road, Hazratganj, Lucknow

SHIVAAZ RESTAURANT 2398667
Opp. Nagar Nigam, 21398668
Off. Vinay Khand, Gomti Nagar,
Lucknow

MOTI MAHAL 2623575
75, Hazratganj, Lucknow 9415024144

AURA LOUNGE 305307475
3rd Floor, Fun Republic, Gomti Nagar,
Lucknow

ARYANS RESTAURANT 2236000
(YASH FOODS) 2230499
C-90, M.G. Marg, Hazratganj, Lucknow

BABIAN CHINESE RESTAURANTS
B-155, Bhootnath, Indiranagar, Lucknow

BIKANERVALA 4064100
B-15, Bhootnath Mod, 4064200
Faizabad Road, Indira Nagar, Lucknow

ARIHANT RESTAURANT 9415066654
Gole Market, Mahanagar, Lko. 9335735554

BHARAT RESTAURANT AND HOTEL
Charbagh, Lucknow 3268053
(OUTDOOR CATERING AVAILABLE) 4048130

THE CLASSIC RESTAURANT 2379938
(Fast Food and Shakes) 2380548
M-28, Ground Floor, Classic Chauraha,
Mahanagar, Lucknow

SPICY BITE RESTAURANT 2617373
Shahnajaf Road, Lucknow 2621622

PACK N CHEW RESTAURANT 9358512939
Vijay Khand, Gomti Nagar, Lucknow

RITZ RESTAURANT 2381090
M-19, Gole Market, Mahanagar, Lucknow 4025101

THE TREAT RESTAURANT 2387532
Shri Ved Prakash Gupta 2387559
M-28 1st Floor, Classic Chauraha,
Mahanagar, Lucknow

WE 2 RESTAURANT 2391195
Shri Manoj Singh
2/53, Vijay Khand, Gomti Nagar,
Lucknow
Birthday, Marriage Anniversary,
Kitty Parties Conferences, etc.

READYMADE GARMENTS
STD CODE - 0522

AWANTI 2620888
54, Halwasia Market, Hazratganj, Lucknow

SANSKRITI 2210526
11, Shahnazaf Road, Hazratganj, Lucknow

AAVARAN 2380205
9-M, Gole Market, Mahanagar, Lucknow

BHASINS COLLECTION 2271311
25, Hazratganj, Lucknow

GINZA MARKETING 2342603
Shop No. 307, IIIrd Floor,
Sahara Shopping Centre, Faizabad Road,
Lucknow

LAMBA AND LAMBA 2274984
40B, Janpath Market, Hazratganj,
Lucknow

LEVI'S 4008284
Shop No. 110, 1st Floor, Saharaganj,
Lucknow

STEAL FACETS CLOTHING CO. 4011380
565, Kha/99, Kanpur Road, Adjacent
Kenara Bank, Alambagh, Luckow

GARHA BHANDAR 2629137
Jhande Wala Park, Aminabad, Lucknow

LAXMI BHANDAR 2624596
20, Aminabad Park, Lucknow

FASHION WEAR (KIDS) 2007020
G-5, Katyani Market, Near B- Block
Crosing, Indira Nagar, Lucknow

PROFILE MENS WEAR 2310939
S-136, Sahara Shopping Centre,
Faizabad Road, Lucknow.

NOOPUR GARMENT 9415424699
Jain Complex, Bhootnath Market,
Lucknow

WILLS LIFESTYLE 2230703
Wills Lifestyle No. 36, Jwala Sahai
Triveni Building, Hazratganj, Lucknow

SUPREME EMPORIUM 4004267
36, Janpath Market, Basement, 2373286
Hazratganj, Lucknow

GARHA BHANDAR 2629137
Jhande Wala Park, Aminabad, Lucknow

RAJ COLLECTIONS 2373286
Shop No. B-9, Arif Chambers,
Kapoorthala Bagh, Lucknow

GINZA MARKETING 2342603
Shop No. 307, IIIrd Floor,
Sahara Shopping Centre, Faizabad Road,
Lucknow

DON'T MISS IN LUCKNOW

•Charbagh Railway Station • Laxman Tila • National Botanical Garden • Saadat Ali Maqbara • Chhattar Manzil

- Saheed Smarak • The Prince University • K.G.M.U • Vidhan Sabha • Mahaveer Tample • Musa Bagh • Moti Mahal
- Ambedkar Park • Anandi Mata Mandir (Chowk) • Anandi Water Park • Indira Gandhi Planetarium • Lohia Park
- Mankameshwar Mandir (Daliganj) • Hanuman Mandir (University Road) • Baba Bhoot Nath Mandir (Indira Nagar)
- Kali Mandir (Kaisarbagh) Swami Aiyappa Mandir (Gomti Nagar) • Gurudwara (Bans Mandi) • Cathedral Church (Cantt.)
- Shani Mandir (Behind Hotel Clarks Avadh) • Dilkusha Garden (Cantt.) • N.B.RI. Ambedkar Maidan • Kukrail Picnic Spot
- Scientific Convention Centre • Spensers for Shopping

REASONABLE AFFORDABLE HOTELS

AC Rooms Double	Rs. 900
Air Cooled SD Single	Rs. 500
Air Cooled SD Double	Rs. 600
Air Cooled Deluxe Single	Rs. 350
Air Cooled Deluxe Double	Rs. 450
Ordinary Room Single	Rs. 275
Ordinary Room Double	Rs. 350
Extra Person	Rs. 75

HOTEL NAZNIN PALACE

Check out Time 24 Hours
38, Cantt. Road, Opp. Harmain Hospital,
Lucknow. Ph. : 0522-2621175, 3204224
E-mail: rafat@hotelnaznlnpalace.com
Website: www.hotelnazninpalace.com

Super Delux Bed	Rs. 1350
Suite	Rs. 1800
Super Deluxe AC Doube	Rs. 1250

Super Deluxe AC Single	Rs. 1110
AC Executive Double	Rs. 950
AC Executive Single	Rs. 800
Air Cooled Double	Rs. 600
Air Cooled Single	Rs. 500
Air Cooled Single	Rs. 400

HOTEL EXPRESS

Check out Time 24 Hours
Hahi Complex, Gurudwara Road,
Basmandi, Lucknow.
Ph.: 0522-2685400
Fax: 0522-2685500

Super Deluxe AC	Rs. 1400
Deluxe AC	Rs. 1250
Extra Person	Rs. 300

VAISHALI HOTEL

(Check-out Time 24 Hours)
1 Sriram Road, Nr. Aminabad Thana, Lko.
Phone: 0522-2684193 M : 9838828266

AC Semi Deluxe (Single)	Rs. 950
AC Semi Deluxe (Double)	Rs. 1100
AC Deluxe (Single)	Rs. 1100
AC Deluxe (Double)	Rs. 1275
Ordinary Room Attached	Rs. 100
Extra Person AC	Rs. 250
Single Room Attached	Rs. 125
Air Cooled	Rs. 150
Air Cooled Room Double	Rs. 250
(Attached with TV)	Rs. 290
AC Rooms Double	Rs. 550

HOTEL MAYUR

(Check-out Time 24 Hours)
Close to Railway Station, Charbagh, Lucknow.
Phone: 0522-4048129,2451824

Non-Attach - Single	Rs. 225

Non-Attach - Double	Rs. 300
Ordinary - Single	Rs. 275
Ordinary - Double	Rs. 350
Deluxe - Single	Rs. 350
AC Deluxe Single	Rs. 450
AC Deluxe - Double	Rs. 550
AC Deluxe Single	Rs. 650
Extra Person	Rs. 100/75

HOTEL SARANG

(Check-out Time 24 Hours)
126/21, Opp. Islamia Coll., B.N. Verma Road
Phone: 0522-2617273, M: 9935403111

Super Deluxe (Double)	Rs. 950
AC Executive Room	Rs. 850
Air Cooled Room	Rs. 350
Air Cooled (Double)	Rs. 600

HOTEL MEZBAAN

(Check-out Time 24 Hours)
92, G.B. Marg, Old RTO, Lko.
Phone: 0522-2202953,3950684

Deluxe Air Cooled (Single)	Rs. 500
Deluxe Air Cooled (Double)	Rs. 600
AC Deluxe - Single	Rs. 800
Air Cooled (Double)	Rs. 900
AC Super Deluxe (Single)	Rs. 900
AC Super Deluxe (Double)	Rs. 1100

Extra Person 20 per cent of Room rent

HOTEL ANANT

(Check-out Time 24 Hours)
16, V.S. Marg, Lucknow
Ph.: 0522-3012209, 3013933

AC Room (Single)	Rs. 700
AC Room (Double)	Rs. 850
Air Cooled Room (Single)	Rs. 350
Air Cooled Room (Double)	Rs. 400

Ordinery (Single)	Rs. 250
Ordinery (Double)	Rs. 300

Extra Person 20 per cent of Room rent

UDAI RAJ LAWN

(Check-out Time 24 Hours)
8, A.P. Sen Road, Charbagh Lko.
Phone: 0522-2630901-3

Semi Deluxe AC Room (Single)	Rs. 800
Semi Deluxe AC Room (Double)	Rs. 1000
Deluxe Room (Single)	Rs. 1000
Deluxe Room (Double)	Rs. 1200
Super Deluxe (Single)	Rs. 1200
Super Deluxe (Double)	Rs. 1550
Suit Room (Single)	Rs. 2000
Suit Room (Double)	Rs. 2000
Extra Person	Rs. 300

SYONA RESIDENCY

(Check-out Time 24 Hours)
82, Charbagh, Kanpur Road, Lucknow
Phone: 0522-2464644 Fax - 0522-1022633

AC Room Single	Rs. 1050
AC Room Double	Rs. 1250
Super Deluxe	Rs. 1500
Executive Room	Rs. 1850
Suite Room	Rs. 2500
Extra Person	Rs. 250

HOTEL GALAXY INTERNATIONAL

(Check-out Time 24 Hours)
Naka Hindola Crossing, Charbagh, Lko.
Phone: 0522-2683201 Fax: 0522-2683405

Air Cooled Room (Single)	Rs. 500
Air Cooled Room (Double)	Rs 600
AC Room (Single)	Rs. 800
AC Room (Double)	Rs. 950

AC Semi Deluxe (Single)	Rs. 950
AC Semi Deluxe (Double)	Rs. 1100
AC Deluxe (Single)	Rs. 1100
AC Deluxe (Double)	Rs. 1275
Extra Person AC	Rs. 250
Air Cooled	Rs. 150

HOTEL AMBER

(Check-out Time 24 Hours)

Ph.: 0522-6450831, 2692371

AC Executive Single	Rs. 2500
AC Executive Double	Rs. 3000
AC Deluxe Single	Rs. 1200
AC Room Double	Rs. 1500
AC Room Single	Rs. 800

28

The Two Clans

Oudh Lucknow or Nucklow, as Kipling called it, has always been much favored by romance and with reason since the days of the viziers of Oudh and the still more famous Begums who has negotiated with Warren Hastings with emerald and rubies to the famous. Begum Hazrat Mahal who had issued the counter proclamation to Queen Victoria's proclamation in India which are all history.

Lucknow; however is not an old city as many other Indian cities are. In fact, it is of a recent and humble origin. In mediaeval times, Lucknow was most likely a collection of scattered villages, and quite unimportant to the Subbah of Avadh. During the Mughal period two clans inhabited the area now known as Lucknow-the Sheikhs and the Pathans came from Ramnagar. The line dividing the territories between the clans was roughly Victoria Street, now known as Tulsidas Marg. East of Victoria Street was the territory of the Sheikhs and the west of it was that of the Pathans.

There was very little habitation outside the area known as the Chowk. In 1540 Humayun came to Lucknow on retreat after defeat by Sher Shah at Jaunpur and he stopped here for about four hours and the Shaikhs collected rupees ten thousand in cash and 50 horses and presented these to him. Earlier the celebrated Sufi Saint Shah Meena had come to Lucknow and died here in 1478 and is buried near Medical College. For long time Lucknow was therefrom known as Meena Nagar. Akbar maintained the copper mint established in the south of Chowk. Mirza Salim who later became Jahangir, also visited Lucknow and founded Mirza Mandi and Akbari Darwaza is also supported to date from the same period.

During Akbar's reign Sheikh Abdur Rahim was the Subedar of Avadh and he also held a Jagir in Bahraich. His tomb is now known as Nidan Mahal or more commonly, Nadan Mahal. In the same area lie the tombs of his father Ibrahim Chisti as well as of others. But for the tomb of Shah Meena this is the oldest building in the city of Lucknow. It was the fashion of these times to construct all worthwhile buildings in stone and constructions of brick were considered in Nadan Mahal are, therefore of stone which must have been imported with considerable difficulty from distances, for no stone is found in the vicinity of Lucknow and the closest in the vicinity of Lucknow and the closest quarries are those at Banda or Kalpi. These buildings are modest compared to the magnificent splendour of similar tombs at Delhi or Agra, and the decoration is also meager.

The next building in historical order is the Teelewali Masjid, which was constructed under the instructions of Aurangzeb on the high mound adjacent to the mound of Machchhi Bhawan. When he happened to pass through Lucknow in a mohalla known as

Alamgirganj, later changed to Aam Nagar, it was founded in his honour.

On the extensive mound which is now occupied by the buildings of the Medical College and the Gandhi Memorial and Associated Hospital, were two famous buildings known as Panch Mahal or five stoned building and Mubarak Mahal. These buildings stood along with their extensive courts and quarters and are the next in historical importance. These were ultimately demolished during the disturbances of 1857.

When Saadat Ali Khan, the first Nawab of Avadh, came to Lucknow and subjugated the Sheikhs who occupied these buildings, he rented them in 1782 on a rent of Rs. 565 a month but he never paid the rent nor did successor Safdar Jung, who secured ownership of these buildings by giving about a thousand *bighas* of land near Dugawan to the previous owners. A picture of Panch Mahal was painted by Thomas William Daniel in the first quarter of the nineteenth century and it shows the sample proportions of this stately mansion.

Soon after he started constructing imposing buildings and set up the Roomi Darwaza, the big Imambara and the mosque attached to it and also constructed the Bibiapur House as a country residence, the Chinhat House, which no longer exists and the Aishbagh pavilion which today has fallen down, only Kothi Bibiapur exists and is in a fairly good state of preservation. It was originally decorated with beautiful tiles from France and has also the oldest spiral staircase in northern India. The staircase has a central shaft of wood and wooden planks for steps.

The Roomi Darwaza and Imambara were completed in the year 1784 at a cost of about one crore of rupees and the plan was drawn up by Kifayatullah. One of the courtiers of Asaf-ud-daula was the famous Frenchman Calude Martin who, as a result of private trade and other resource, had earned great wealth. Claude Martin built a house on the river with main gates on the Chhatar Manzil and Farhat Bux Palace. He also built Constantia known as La Martiniere College but he died before he could shift to it.

Soon after succeeding to the Nawabi of Avadh, Asaf-ud-daula also started constructing the Residency for the representatives of the East India Company who had securely bound him with the treaties and pledges of tribute and these buildings were almost completed by 1780.

The architectural remains of the period ending with Asaf-ud-daula's reign are not considerable and have generally been considered inferior to comparable architectural activity of the contemporary period elsewhere. There is a considerable amount of truth in it for there is lack of vigor of integrated symmetry in these buildings. Nevertheless this era is closely related to the life and culture of the times and no one can dispute the excellence of craftsmanship and skill in execution. The Imambara has the largest unsupported vaulted roof in the world, and the Roomi Darwaza is still the most imposing gate in Lucknow.

29

Lucknow My Lucknow

Rohin Arora

Touch down

The only change in the Airport was the change of name since I last visited the city of Nawabs: Amausi Airport had given way to Chaudhary Charan Singh International Airport. I remember the name being changed by the center during the trust vote over nuclear deal so as to get Ajit Singh to vote in favour of UPA. Ajit Singh and voting and cash for votes scandal had come into limelight a couple of months ago through Wikileaks. Lucknow airport had found no mention in wikileaks as this perhaps was the legal bribery. Ajit Singh finally didn't vote for UPA but Lucknow airport did get a new name.

Paradise after Chaos

As you hit the Kanpur road, you know you are in Lucknow. The streets were chaotic with each vehicle trying to hit the other vehicles on the road. Most vehicles were on the wrong side of the road and were pretty comfortable with the idea. All cars, buses and tempo drivers had their one hand on the horn. My taxi driver maneuvered the cab erratically missing a few tempos and rickshaws by a whisker. I couldn't believe that he did not hit anything on the way. I prepared myself for 30 minutes of chaos when suddenly the cab turned right and we were on swanky new road. On the sides were neat sandstone walls enclosing huge parks. The walls carried on and on and so did the parks. It was a never ending. It all looked pretty majestic. From the cab one could see some monuments and statues inside the parks. These parks had names like 'Eco Park', 'Buddha Sthal' and 'Kanshi Ram Park'. It was tempting to just stop and look inside but I knew that a few minutes will not do justice to these miles and miles of parks. I promised to return when weather was better as these parks looked good for a more detailed visit.

Food Fit for Nawabs

It was already 7 PM by the time I reached home, so didn't feel like going to Chowk or Nazirabad for Tundey kababs in this heat so went to Sapru Marg to their new outlet. Had a couple of Kababs there itself and packed some Mutton Korma, Biryani, Boti Kabab, Shammi Kababs and Sheermals to be had in air conditioning comfort of home while watching an IPL match. As always, the food was amazing. This kind of preparation is difficult to get anywhere else but Lucknow. Korma is relatively less oily than what you get in Delhi; Kababs melt in your mouth; and the smell of Biryani makes you open the box on the way to the house and taste a bit. Not only was this my meal for the next night also but I carried all this stuff to Delhi as well. As always, my friends in Delhi waited for me to come back with this Avadhi food.

Gunj and Gunjing

Hazratganj, the main market of Lucknow took me with a lot of surprise. My association with Gunj (popular name for Hazratganj) was not restricted to Gunjing (during our time this meant-roaming in Hazratganj and looking at girls from Loreto and La Martiniere girls), or watching English movies at Mayfair. My grandfather and father had a shop called 'Modern Novelties' in the heart of Hazratganj and this shop remained one of the landmarks of Lucknow till it shut down more than a decade back. It sold everything- cosmetics, packaged food, imported items (a big attraction in 70's), chocolates, poultry products, video films, music, hot dogs, ham, sausages and even turkey at Christmas time.

There were many small kiosks in the same lane making it a very tight lane to walk in. This lane was known as 'lovers lane' (for obvious reasons!) till the kiosks were broken down and alternate shops were allotted to the kiosk owners at the newly created Janpath market.

The controversial Ambedkar Park in Gomti Nagar across from Taj had just been a trailer for things to come as far as Mayawati was concerned. Ambedkar Park was created during her last reign. On coming back to power, Gomti Nagar went for a metamorphosis. I certainly could not believe what I saw of Gomti Nagar. Broad roads, many flyovers, upmarket restaurants, big malls and fancy shops seem to have come from nowhere. But what took the cake was the glittering Gomti Nagar at night. The breathtaking lights adorning the Ambedkar park and its million statues; colourful fountains; broad avenues well lighted up; and once again that sandstone look with which we identify Rashtrapati Bhavan and India Gate. It all looked spectacular! Paris would soon face competition from Gomti Nagar for the name of 'city of lights'.

Maya Behnji

The Maya magic seemed to have worked in the then Lucknow. People generally seemed to be happy with what she did. They are quite proud of the new look Lucknow Hazratganj. They felt that she was despotic and autocratic but then the improvement in law and order compensated for a lot of flaws. Her banners and her statues were everywhere. The people felt that Congress had no chance so why to waste the vote. Mulayam Singh and Samajwadi party could make a comeback in other parts of U.P. but stood no chance in Lucknow. It seemed unlikely that anyone could topple the Queen from her throne for in the next few years.

Now the Mulayam Singh and Samajwadi Party government have come back to power with his son Akhilesh Singh as the Chief Minister. The heat is on for the General Elections of 2014 works as UP results are important.

It is not that Lucknow and its people have changed completely. The traffic is still chaotic; the sidewalks and buildings are still stained red with paan spit'; and dirt and filth is still a major feature in many areas. The elegant havelis are giving way to ugly multi storied structures. The heat and paucity of time did not allow me to visit my alma mater, La Martiniere College or the Old Lucknow or any of the clubs. In the 40 odd hours I had seen quite enough. Sitting in a fancy lounge bar, I considered having a beer. As the waiter took the order, I changed my mind. The occasion demanded something stronger!

30

Mahomed Bagh Club

History of Club

"Lucknow Hum Par Fida, Aur Hum Fidae Lucknow
Kya Haisiyat Aasmaan Ki Jo Churaye Lucknow"

(We are all for Lucknow and Lucknow is all for us;

The heavens have no authority to deprive us of Lucknow)

This is how the generations have related to the City of Lucknow ...!

History of The Mahomed Bagh Club's intriguingly associated with that of Lucknow, and thus it would not be out of context to peep in to various stages of the city's past to descend at the point in time when The Mahomed Bagh Club came into existence.

Lucknow developed as the center of art, culture, attire and etiquette ("Tehzeeb" and was called "Paris of the east". In fact, the bridge over river Gomti near famous monument "Bara Imambara" built by Nawab Asaf-ud-daula in late 16th century is a replica of a River Scene in Paris. This was around the time when European

Architecture entered India, and the Nawabs of Avadh, afforded its due share.

Avadh Province was ruled by the "Shaikhzadas", till 1722, when Saadat Ali Khan was appointed its Governor. He introduced the "Two fish" symbol as the official logo that continues till date as the official logo of UP Govt. MB Club logo incorporated the fishes around 'MBC' in early 80's to compliment its heritage.

The Nawabi rule lasted till 1856. East India Company took over Avadh in 1764, with the defeat of Shuja-ud-Daula. His son Asaf-ud-daula permanently shifted the capital from Faizabad to Lucknow. He is credited with Lucknow's development as the city of palaces and gardens. The "Bara Imambara" or "Bhool Bhulaiyan" was built by him during the famine. It has one of the largest vaulted galleries in the world. The last of the dynasty was Nawab Wajid Ali Shah, a connoisseur of fine arts, performing arts, poetry and the attendant vices. He built the "Kesarbagh" Palace complex at Qaiser Bagh, to accommodate his various concubines.

Nawab Saadat Ali Khan built a string of gardens and orchards right from the old city to the outskirts. He built Dilkusha Palace/Garden on Sultanpur road as a picnic/recreation resort for Nawabs and their guests. Dilkusha pocket of Lucknow had an orchard named Mahomed Bagh. The British Government after taking over the reigns from East India Company in 1856 established the Lucknow Cantonment- post mutiny, in these surroundings.

Mahomed Bagh, along with its structures built by the British Army was chosen as the venue for the blue British club and named Mahomed Bagh Club Ltd., established for promotion of games, amusement, social and literary enjoyment for its members and their families, the management committee of the club consisting of army officers executed a Deed with Bank of Upper India Ltd. For a princely sum of Rs. 28,000 on 20th October 1899, at interest @ 8 per cent per annum, to create various facilities for the members.

A Memorandum and Articles of Association and the Bylaws evolved as the base for club's functioning. Originally the membership was open only to defence service officers. In 1947, the club started accepting civil services officers, Taluqdars, the Feudal class and other prominent citizen as members. The ICS and IPD cadre was granted only temporary membership. Gradually more civilian members were inducted. Membership of the club was frozen for about a decade and restarted in end of 2000, with modified registration and membership process, and permission of the Company Law Board to increase the upper limit to 2350 members.

Traditionally the GOC-in-C, Central Command, Lucknow is the Patron. Chairmanship of the club rotates between the Chief of Staff, Central Command and the Chief Secretary U.P. Govt. on yearly basis. Till 1971, a serving officer looked after the club as its honorary secretary. The club opted for a full time paid secretary since, and a retired Lt. Col is usually appointed.

The club had a typical "Brit" culture till the early years of independence, duly inherited from the people who brought the concept of clubs in the country. The Burma Teak floored ballroom with live band on the stage used to be inviting enough to go to the floor and Waltz. The stage was extensively used for plays at one time. Ballroom was the venue for Dance Eves, with sitting arrangements in the adjoining Bar and other compartments.

In early 80's such functions had to move out of doors to accommodate more participants. The cemented Badminton Court on the side lawns served the purpose of dance floor - liberally sprinkled with French chalk. The floor has gradually been expanded and the French chalk is passe now, because 'gliding' on the floor has been replaced by gymnastics type of dancing.

The dress code imbibed from those years continues. Kurtas, and Collarless T-shirts are not permitted. The tops must be tucked in. Decent jeans are now permitted. Formal functions like the dance eves strictly prescribe the DJ or Lounge suit. After independence the Official Indian equivalents of the DJ like the Nehru Jacket and Sherwani with trouser are accepted.

The good old covered swimming pool which lay empty for several years is now being built into an air conditioned banquet hall. The Olympic size pool across the road, was renovated and upgraded by the club with modern filtration plant and machinery, for the benefit of the members and their families.

The pool side lawn is popular venue for parties also, during the off season. A health club has been developed on top of the pool building. The club has many affiliations all over the country and abroad.

Facilities provided include seven bungalows, three transit cottages, library, air conditioned bars, family lounge with party rooms, dining hall, billiards, card rooms, the ballroom, semi-circular front lawn, side lawn with bar and outdoor kitchen at its two ends, tennis courts, walkers' track, children's play park, staff quarters, florist shop, etc. Tambola is held every Sunday in the air conditioned ballroom and is moved out to the front lawn during winters. The club has always been a venue for quality entertainment like Fashion shows and Concerts by renowned artistes.

Located in the greenest belt of the city, with abundance of natural beauty and wide open areas, the club has maintained its old dignified charm, while adopting modern facilities over the years, and is one of the best known residential clubs, among the traditional clubs that were established by the British.

The Lucknow 'andaaz'- a style and spirit is prevalent at the Mahomed Bagh Club.

Index